Will the Real
Gertrude Hollings
Please Stand Up?

Jennifer
Hattingh
Z

Will the Real
Gertrude Hollings
Please Stand Up?

Sheila Greenwald

A Yearling Book

Published by
Dell Publishing Co., Inc.
1 Dag Hammarskjold Plaza
New York, New York 10017

Yearling® TM 913705, Dell Publishing Co., Inc.

ISBN: 0-440-49553-9

Reprinted by arrangement with Little, Brown and Company in association
with the Atlantic Monthly Press
Printed in the United States of America

May 1985

10 9 8 7 6 5 4 3 2

CW

For Alison Morss

Will the Real
Gertrude Hollings
Please Stand Up?

❧ One ❧

WHEN Gertrude let herself into her apartment, smelled a delicious roast, saw her mother's briefcase on the hall bench and the dining-room table set for six instead of three, she wondered if by some miracle the day might have reversed itself and become good.

"Who's coming for dinner?" She hurried into the kitchen.

Mrs. Hollings looked up from the roast she was prodding and closed the oven. Her face was pink and glowing. "Aunt Eugenia, Uncle Bruce, and . . ."

"And Albert," Gertrude completed the sentence with dramatic disgust. "Are we celebrating? Did you finish the article?"

"I did, but there's more than that. Something very exciting has happened." Mrs. Hollings's high spirits seemed to fill the kitchen as much as the smell of browning onions.

"Tell me." Gertrude fell onto a red stool and began to nibble some carrots that had been cut for a salad.

"The magazine has asked me to do a piece for them on Greece." Mrs. Hollings pulled her dark hair back from her face and wiped her hands on a towel. "By an amazing coincidence the network wants Daddy to fly to Athens to film a special. Can you imagine? We get to go together." She clapped her hands in delight and noticed her watch. "I'll tell you all about our exciting plans for you, Gerts, but I'm running late. It'll have to be a surprise until dinner. Could you help me out and tidy up the bathroom before they come? I expect them any minute."

Gertrude went happily into her room. She loved surprises when they were good, and she never had bad ones at home. Home was her safe place. When she was there, she was the Gertrude who was loved and bright. She was not "dork" or "simp" or "dumbhead." She had no labels. She put her knapsack on her bed, sat down beside it, letting the school Gertrude slip away, and sighed with the pleasure her room always evoked in her.

An article in the magazine her mother worked for had advised that it helped to organize a room if you gave it a theme. It wasn't hard to figure out what Gertrude's theme was. There were owls on her bedspread, owls on her lampshade and owls all over her new wallpaper. She went to the shelf where her collection of stuffed owls were arranged and picked them up one at a time. Olivia, a beautiful white velvet snowy, imported from Germany, had huge innocent black eyes made of glass and real eyelashes. Oliver was soft brown felt with rubbery feet. His feathers were handpainted in Japan. Aster and Oster were an old married pair made of plush. Their three babies, Ring, Ding and Ping, were plastic. Gertrude carried them all to her bed. She placed Olivia on the pillow. "I have very good news," she said. "We are going to Greece."

"Can you fit us in your suitcase?" Olivia asked in the high crooning voice Gertrude used for her. "Will you show us the town?"

"I may be very busy," Gertrude said. "I'll probably have to help my parents with their work."

"What about school?" Aster said sourly.

"Hah." Gertrude flopped back and hugged herself. "I'm freeeeee." She could practically feel herself flying so high that her entire world was like a dot on the ground, miles below. "I'm flying away from it." She laughed out loud at the thought. Away from homework she couldn't do and teachers she couldn't like and classmates she couldn't befriend and a part in drama she couldn't learn. . . . Away.

The front door slammed. Her father's greeting rang through the apartment. "Hello . . . The Nugents are with me. We all came up together."

Gertrude sat up and guiltily remembered she had forgotten to tidy the bathroom. She would fly away from tidying bathrooms too.

She ran to greet her father.

"Hey, how's my one and only Gertie?" Mr. Hollings gave Gertrude his happiest twirling hug. He seemed as excited as her mother.

Even Eugenia and Bruce, who were usually reserved, had caught some of the mood, for they were talking all at once.

Albert pulled at Gertrude's elbow. "Do you have a deck of cards?"

"Why?" She began to shake him off but changed her mind. After all, she was the one going to Greece. Why not be nice to Albert?

"I am the casino champ of my class," Albert boasted.

"I don't play casino."

"How about hearts?"

"I don't play cards."

"Boy, it's going to be a rough three weeks."

"What do you mean?"

His mouth was full of nuts. "Checkers? Do you play checkers?"

"Chess," Gertrude said. "I like chess."

"That's the one I hate." Albert thrust his hand back into the bowl of nuts. Gertrude knew that he wouldn't play chess with her because she had taught him the moves and then beat him at the game just last Christmas.

"Okay, let's play checkers." Gertrude led him to her room.

When Albert saw the stuffed owls on her bed, he pointed at them and rolled his eyes. "Oh nooo, you don't still play with stuffed animals?"

"I was just arranging them," she said, quickly sweeping the birds into a drawer in her night table. She set the checkerboard on her bed.

"I like red," Albert said, taking the red pieces. "Red goes first."

"Sure. Go first at checkers, Albert." Gertrude smiled graciously. She singsonged, "You don't go first to Greece."

"To Greece?" Albert frowned. "What are you talking about?"

"Never mind," Gertrude said. She didn't want to rub it in.

He moved his piece out and Gertrude did the same. Before long Albert was building little towers of the black pieces he had taken from her on his side of the board. "Your move." He watched carefully as she picked up a black disk and set it down again. "Don't do that," he barked. "I'll take your man again. You aren't paying any attention. You keep leaving yourself open. If I win, you won't want to play anymore."

"Would that be so bad?"

"Believe me, there isn't much else to do at Hillside."

"Hillside?"

"Our house in the country. There's no TV. One whole week at Hillside over spring vacation is two hundred and sixty checkers games."

"Poor Albert." Gertrude sighed for him. "Is that where you're going for your spring vacation? Hillside?"

"We've got records and jigsaw puzzles and Parcheesi."

Albert's face twitched. "But that's about it. If it rains it seems like months instead of a week."

Gertrude shook her head gleefully. "I'd just die of boredom."

"Don't do that, we have no cemetery."

"I'll send you a postcard." She laughed.

"From the grave?" He took up his piece and jumped her last three men. "Sorry."

"I told you. I never win with black."

He drew a red plastic wallet out of his pocket and removed a piece of paper from it. With a pencil stub, he jotted on the paper. "I'll keep track of our scores. After three weeks we'll know who is the champ."

Three weeks? Whatever was Albert talking about? Even though she couldn't stand Albert, Gertrude was sorry to observe that he had finally lost his marbles completely.

When they were called in for dinner, Albert smirked and said to his parents, "Guess what? Gertie still plays with stuffed animals."

"Now Albert," Aunt Eugenia warned.

"She does. I saw them on her bed. She had them all out. She doesn't play cards. She's terrible at checkers and she plays with baby toys. What kind of fun will that be?"

Gertrude saw her mother's face stiffen. "Remember how you used to plead with Gertie to make up stories with those stuffed owls? It wasn't that long ago, Albert."

Albert scrunched his eyebrows together and twitched his nose up and down.

"You called them Owl Games, O.G.s," Gertrude reminded him.

"I was just a baby then," he said to his plate. "Now I'm the casino champ of my class. I'm on the soccer team too." His entire face was beset by three separate tics: his eyebrows wriggled, his nose went up and down, and his mouth darted over to one side. It was like a ballet.

Mrs. Hollings put the roast on the sideboard and began to slice it. "I hope a leg of lamb is all right, Eugenia," she said. "I didn't ask if you had begun to crave strange foods."

"Peanut butter and pickles?" Eugenia laughed.

"Maybe it will be a girl this time," Mrs. Hollings said.

Gertrude looked from one to the other. It suddenly dawned on her that her Aunt Eugenia was expecting a baby. Perhaps that accounted for Albert's new tics and the odd things he had said. She decided to listen very hard so that she could understand what was going on and avoid asking a dumb question.

Eugenia closed her eyes and sighed. "Are you already preparing for Greece?"

"I've got to take clothes to the cleaners and get my passport renewed." Mrs. Hollings nodded. "There isn't much time."

Gertrude could no longer stand the suspense. "When do we go?" she burst.

"We?" Albert hooted. "You aren't going, stupid. You're coming to stay with us."

Eugenia looked up with an expression of shock. "Doesn't Gertie know?"

Mrs. Hollings's cheeks flushed to the color of brick. "It was so sudden. We just learned at two o'clock this afternoon. Gertie got home late. I was going to talk to her before you came."

"You prepare a child for something like this, Dora," Eugenia interrupted. "You don't just spring it on her. Good grief."

Gertrude saw her mother shrink. She felt as if she were shrinking herself, as if she were folding up and disappearing.

Eugenia turned to Gertrude, her eyes large and kindly. "Your parents are going to be away for three weeks, Gertie. You will stay with us. We'll spend two weeks in the city, and then, as it will be spring vacation, we'll go up to our house at Hillside for the third week. We'll also spend the weekends there. The four of us are going to have a wonderful time."

"When are you leaving?" Gertrude asked her mother in a voice that wobbled.

"Next Monday." Mrs. Hollings began to cough nervously.

Suddenly Gertrude realized the day had not reversed itself by any miracle. Not at all. It had, as she might have expected, gone from bad to worse to horrid within a few brief moments.

❧ *Two* ❧

WHEN her aunt and uncle and cousin had left, Mr. Hollings hugged Gertrude. "Don't be angry, sweetie."

"Oh Gertie, I feel rotten," her mother said. "It's just that it all happened so fast."

Gertrude shook her head. "But I don't want to live with them. Why can't you take me with you?"

Mr. and Mrs. Hollings exchanged unhappy glances. "We'll be working hard. It wouldn't be much fun for you. This isn't a family trip."

"I understand that," Gertrude said. "I don't mind. I'd keep busy. I would play by myself in the hotel room. I could even help you with your work."

Mrs. Hollings stopped putting dishes in the washer. "It's the first time we've gone away without you. It's hard for us, too. But don't you think it's important for us to find out that we can live without each other for a while?" She didn't wait for Gertrude to answer. "We've always been so close. This is good preparation."

"For what?"

"For the years to come. Our lives will take us away from each other. The more we learn how to do it, the better we'll get."

"Who'll rehearse me for my part of Tituba?" Gertrude wailed, "And who'll water the plants?"

"Mrs. Tansey next door will take our plants into her living room and keep an eye on the apartment for us," Mrs. Hollings assured her. "And I'm certain Aunt Eugenia would love to help you learn your lines for the play."

Gertrude went back to her room. The owls that had given her such pleasure only a few hours ago stared reproachfully from the night-table drawer where she had dumped them. She put on her pajamas and carried the birds to their shelf.

"I have terrible news," Gertrude said.

Immediately Olivia began to sneeze from her allergy. "Don't tell me. I can't bear it."

"You must all be very brave."

"I can't be brave," Aster replied. "It's bad for me."

"What is it, Gertrude?" Oliver asked.

"I will have to leave you for three weeks while I go to stay with Albert and his parents."

"Oh doe," Olivia sobbed. "I thought we were all going to Greece."

"I thought so, too."

"Take us with you?" Oster suggested brightly.

Gertrude shook her head. "This is not a family vacation. You heard Albert. He would torment us all."

"I can't bear it," Olivia whimpered.

"You will have to bear it and so will I. Maybe it will even do us good."

"How can you say that, Gertrude?"

"It will be a preparation," she said slowly, "for the times ahead when we will be separated from each other."

"This is tragic." Olivia sighed and shook. Aster and Oster lay on their sides and wept quietly. Ring, Ding and Ping huddled.

Only Oliver stood. "We'll be in each other's thoughts," he said. "When you think of us, Gertie, we'll be there for you. Now go to sleep and remember, you're still Gertrude, no matter where you are. No matter where you go."

Gertrude closed her eyes and thought about this. Still Gertrude? That was hardly a comfort. Who was Gertrude anyway? There was her parents' Gertrude, the owls' Gertrude, the school Gertrude, Albert's Gertrude.

There was Gertrude Hollings who lived on the Upper West Side of Manhattan not far from the university where her Uncle Bruce taught dead languages and her Aunt Eugenia art history. She was only a bus ride away from her third "new school." The schools she had gone to had been both public and private, each had a different name and philosophy of teaching, but there was one thing about them that was always the same. They had been places where Gertrude Hollings was "dumb," as some of her classmates would point out, or "unmotivated," as some of her teachers might say.

Eugenia, Bruce, and Albert Nugent lived only seven blocks away from the Hollingses, but it might as well have been another planet. Most of the time Gertrude wished her cousin Albert was on Mars. A full year younger than Gertrude, he was in the same grade, and he never let her forget it. Albert went to a school where the boys wore blue blazers with the school emblem stitched to the pocket. He wore gray flannel pants with a sharp crease. He set off every morning looking like the "perfect little man." He carried his books in an attaché case. In Albert's school each grade had three sections. Albert was in the "smart fourth." He was given tests on which he got ninety or a hundred and report cards on which he got A's. He had constant proof of his smartness.

Since her new school didn't give grades, Gertrude no longer had to answer to Albert's boasting. She certainly didn't have to tell him about the fat envelope full of written reports that the teachers at Bradwin sent out three times a year, or that she had managed to read one that was lying on her mother's desk. She didn't have to tell Albert that she knew what it had said, though she tried hard to forget.

We are somewhat concerned by Gertrude's lack of motivation. Tutoring appears to be helping her, but her

learning disabilities make it difficult for her to engage
with success in class assignments. She is a sweet child
and is not a behavior problem. We try to avoid assign-
ing her work she cannot handle so that she will not
become frustrated and give up completely. Our unstruc-
tured classes make it possible for us to do this. Gertrude
needs more confidence in her ability to master skills. She
is afraid of being hurt, afraid to get involved and afraid
to fail.

Gertrude Hollings and Albert Nugent.

Learning Disabled and Superachiever.

Her mother had said that staying with the Nugents
would be preparation. Preparation for failing after
school as much as she had failed all day.

❧ *Three* ❧

THERE were good weeks and bad weeks. Gertrude believed that the way a week began was the way it kept going. Better and better or worse and worse. But how, she wondered on a rainy Tuesday in the first week of April, could anything possibly be worse than yesterday? Gazing at a workbook page full of numbers, she realized that she was only halfway through the second day of what was sure to be the worst week of her life.

"Can't you do it?" Jessie Bogues, who sat beside her whispered.

"We didn't have this at my old school."

"You've been at Bradwin since December, Gertie," Jessie reminded her. "Soon *this* will be your old school."

Gertrude covered the workbook page protectively with her arm and began to write numbers in the spaces, imitating an expression of deep concentration. She was a good mimic.

"Which ones can't you do?" Jessie persisted.

Gertrude showed her the page grudgingly. "Number twelve."

"That's not a twelve. It's a twenty-one. You reversed the number." Jessie peered down at the rest of the work. "All your sevens are backwards," she remarked matter-of-factly. "And you've made that six in the first column a nine. You're like my brother Alex. Dyslec . . . something-or-other."

"Jessie, stop bothering Gertrude," the teacher, Mrs. Delson, called.

"I'm not bothering her, I'm helping her."

"I'll do the helping. You do your own work." Mrs. Delson came up behind them and leaned over Gertrude. She took up Gertrude's workbook and puzzled over the page for a moment. Then she carried the book back to her desk where she showed it to Emily, the other group teacher. They talked in low voices.

"Dyslexic, that's it," Jessie said proudly. "You're dyslexic, right?"

Gertrude shrugged. The word always made her nervous.

"Do you see a tutor for it?"

Gertrude nodded dumbly. She was beginning to feel frantic.

"My brother goes three times a week. I work with him at home. I'm very good at helping him. I think it will be my career when I grow up."

"Helping your brother?"

"No," Jessie said impatiently, "tutoring children who have learning disabilities. That's what my mother does. She's got a master's degree in it."

Gertrude felt her pulse throb in her ears, as if she were on a plane. Her eyes played a trick and she could see Jessie all grown up, with her sleek black hair pulled tight back from her perfectly round serious face. A tutor with a master's degree.

Mrs. Delson returned with a mimeographed sheet of paper. "We've decided to take you out of the workbook for the time being, Gertrude. You'll do better using these loose sheets. They'll be your homework."

The words "we're taking you out of the workbook" were familiar. They were the same words her teachers at Partridge Mellon Lower had said only a year ago. "We're taking you out of the workbook" was followed by "We're taking you out of the fourth grade," which was followed by her parents telling her, "We're taking you out of Partridge Mellon Lower." When Gertrude had asked where she would go to school, her mother had cheerfully said, "To Bradwin, darling. They've got art and music and drama. The classes are ungraded and they don't give tests and marks. Bradwin is more free and open than Partridge Mellon. It will be a nice change."

Maybe so. But at the moment Bradwin was beginning to sound very much like Partridge Mellon.

"Are those sheets easier?" Jessie was relentless. "I could help you with them. You could come over to my house after school."

Gertrude made her eyes vacant and turned away. One thing she had learned to do at both schools was avoid her classmates. But Jessica Bogues had been trying to get her attention for weeks. She made a point of sitting beside her on the bus ride home, offered food from her lunchbox, and now was trying to set up an after-school date.

"Do you see your tutor today?"

"I stay for drama."

Jessie was pleased. "So do I. I'll tutor you in the math till it starts." Something occurred to her. "Unless you want me to help you with your lines; you're Tituba, aren't you?"

"Leave Gertrude alone, Jess," Mrs. Delson called.

"I am h-e-l-p-i-n-g her," Jessie muttered under her breath.

❧ Four ❧

GOING to school on the Broadway bus the next morning, Gertrude was lost in an Owl Game. Olivia was flying through Riverside Park at night trying to find the Nugents' apartment, specifically Gertrude's window in that apartment. Someone had spotted Olivia and called the zoo. There were zookeepers with traps searching the city, but even worse, there was the evil impresario Boris Plink, who needed a snowy owl for his Bird Extravaganza. He had placed his agents on the roofs of the tallest buildings overlooking the park. The agents carried nets to drop on Olivia. "Gertrude," Olivia called, "where is your window?"

Jessie Bogues squeezed into the seat beside Gertrude. "Do you realize you were talking to yourself in a public place?"

Gertrude gulped. She quickly looked around her. "I was reminding myself of the things I have to take with me to my aunt's house. I'll be there for three weeks while my parents are in Greece."

"If you stayed at my house, I could tutor you full time. Since you'd be my first client, I wouldn't charge."

"I have a tutor."

"I know that, but more can't hurt. Look, I could coach you for your role in the play and help with your homework too." When Gertrude didn't answer, Jessie went on. "Did you do the math pages Mrs. Delson gave you?"

Gertrude remembered that she had forgotten to take them out of the pocket of her skirt. The skirt had gone into the wash. "Mrs. Delson doesn't usually collect work from me. I'll do it later."

"See, I could have helped you," Jessie said, proving her point. "You know that if you don't remind her, Mrs. Delson will forget." She faced Gertrude squarely. She was serious and disapproving. "At Bradwin the teachers can get very sloppy. If you are not a behavior problem and don't act out, they'll leave you alone and you won't even get your basics. It's up to you to be sure you are learning, Gertrude, believe me. It's your responsibility. And, *I* am the person who can help you." She pulled a felt-tipped pen from her pocket and without even asking permission wrote on Gertrude's canvas knapsack. "I don't have a card yet. That's my phone number."

"Why do you want to tutor me so much?"

"Because you need it." Jessie looked out the bus window. "And so do I. It's my career."

They got off the bus at their stop and walked toward

the school. "I'm so happy I have my future career planned out," Jessie said. "Do you?"

"I don't think about it too much," Gertrude confessed. In fact, she avoided all thoughts of "when I grow up." Mrs. Hollings once told Mr. Hollings, "I'll bet if Gertie had a choice, she'd rather grow down." It was true. She would much rather go back to that happy time before school. Looking ahead to years of unknown events seemed like staring into a dark crater with no bottom.

At lunch she chose her usual corner table. She chose it because nobody sat at it unless they had no other place. The kitchen door kept banging open on one side and the trash can was on the other. Even with the banging and the clanking, Gertrude liked it better than the other tables.

A very thin girl named Nina Godwin approached the trash can and emptied the entire contents of her lunchbox. She did this every day, tossing out the neatly wrapped sandwich and unblemished apple her mother had packed, but today she paused at Gertrude's table. "Is Jessie Bogues after you for some new career project?" she asked Gertrude.

"What do you mean?"

"I can tell when Jessie wants something, and this year it seems to be you. Last year it was me."

"What did she want you for?"

"Her beauty parlor. She got some of us to let her cut

our hair. Mine's still growing out." She tugged on the ragged ends of her thin blond bangs. "Before that Jessie was teaching sex education and tonette. She had five people in her class. Somebody told me she wants to get into private tutoring. Is that you?"

Gertrude saw Jessie enter the lunchroom and look around. She wished it was for someone else, but when Jessie's eyes found her, she smiled and headed for the table.

"I guess I better sit with you. We can get a little vocabulary review in while we eat."

Nina winked. "It *is* you."

How will I survive the *day?* Gertrude wondered, much less three weeks.

Mrs. Daniels who taught drama had red hair and brown eyes. She kept a trunk full of costumes and fake jewelry in the corner of the large basement room where drama classes were held. The contents of the trunk were used on days when the class improvised skits. But today was different. Every spring at Bradwin the drama class rehearsed a short play based on their work in social studies. Since they had been studying colonial times, the play was about the witch trials in Salem Village. To Gertrude's amazement and delight, one week before she had been chosen to play the role of Tituba, a slave accused of witchcraft. It was the biggest girl's part in the play. She had read her lines from a mimeographed script again and again in front of her mirror at home, and to her parents. As she took her seat on the floor in a half-circle around Mrs. Daniels, she remembered that today they would run through their parts on the little stage. She remembered too that she had forgotten her script.

"Tituba," Mrs. Daniels said. As she called each name the student went up on the stage carrying a script. "Tituba, what happened to your script?"

"I don't have my script."

"Here's an extra one." Mrs. Daniels gave her the stapled sheets. "Please remember to bring yours next time."

The minute she began to read her lines Gertrude knew something peculiar was happening.

Chris Kinnel, the narrator, covered his mouth to stop a giggle. Somebody in the audience choked. Gertrude squinted as if there were something wrong with her eyes, and as she tried to focus on the paper she was aware of the actors nudging one another.

"Try it again, Gertrude," Mrs. Daniels said.

"I am no witch, Master. I work hard and bake cook the little girls clean and sweep . . ."

"Gertie puts her words in a blender," Chris whispered to Justin Avery in a voice that carried.

"A food processor," Justin responded.

"A cement mixer," Chris tried again. The laughter that resulted from this was almost welcome to Gertrude. If nothing else, it meant she could stop reading.

"Let's move along to page four," Mrs. Daniels called

in a brisk voice. Gertrude's ears were thrumbing so loudly she couldn't hear the other parts. "Your turn," Chris told her impatiently. She lifted the script nearly to her eyes. She had seen Mrs. Daniels's concerned expression and could feel the heavy silence that anticipated another of her "blended speeches."

Something awful was happening. She was different in a way that people found funny. Why? What was so peculiar about her? The sudden shock of laughter that greeted the things she said gave her a familiar sense of drowning. Glug glug, down down. She hoped it would be over soon and she would be at the bottom where no one would notice anymore.

"Do you want to try it again?" Mrs. Daniels said.

Gertrude shook her head. Who would want to try drowning twice?

As soon as drama was over, Gertrude hurried to find the girls' room. But she couldn't remember where it was. Though she had been at Bradwin for five months, the rooms were suddenly as scrambled as the words of the script had been. She saw a door with red letters on it and went in. It was a washroom with sinks and booths for toilets, but it didn't look familiar. A new bathroom? She went into a booth and sat down. She put her head on the cool wall, letting the memory of the sound of laughter and the throb it made in her brow subside. She heard the door open and the water splash in the sink. She heard the door open again.

"Oh Susan," Mrs. Daniels's voice said.

Gertrude realized with a jolt that she was in the teacher's washroom.

"Helen," Mrs. Delson said in a light voice, "I read the Tituba script and I love it. The story is perfect for our social studies work. The children are having a wonderful time with it."

"It's going very well, except," water splashed, "except for one child, and I just don't know what her trouble is."

"Who's that?"

"Gertrude Hollings. I gave her the role of Tituba, since she was new to the school and seemed a bit shy. She can't seem to learn her lines. It's turning into a real problem."

"Oh, Helen, didn't I tell you about Gertie?"

"No." The water was turned off, and Gertrude feared that they would hear her heart thudding. "What about Gertrude?"

"Why, she's learning disabled. She sees a tutor a few times a week, but progress is s-l-o-w." Mrs. Delson dragged out the word.

"I wish I'd known that," Mrs. Daniels said with feeling. "I would never have given her the lead if I had. I certainly don't wish to humiliate her. Now what do I do? I'll only make it worse if I pull her out."

"I see your point." There was silence for a moment. "Say, what a nice shade of lipstick, Helen. What is it?"

"Pink Magic," Mrs. Daniels said. "I wish I could wave it over Gertie Hollings so she'd learn her lines."

"I'll send a note home to her mother. It would help if her parents would work with her."

"Good idea," Mrs. Daniels said. The water splashed again. Gertrude held her feet up so they wouldn't see her sneakers under the partition.

Her mother and father couldn't help her. They were going to Greece.

She had been laughed at.

They never should have given her the role.

Jessie Bogues was "after her."

And, it was still only Tuesday . . . the Tuesday of the worst week of her life.

❧ Five ❧

THE days till the Hollingses left passed both quickly and slowly. It was endless agony watching the suitcases come down from the top closet shelves and being slowly filled. But it was horribly quick when each morning marked one day less till the dreaded event.

"Are you sure Mrs. Tansey will water the plants?" Gertrude looked out the kitchen window across the courtyard into Mrs. Tansey's kitchen. "Will she keep an eye on things?"

"Don't worry about it, darling. The apartment will be as well looked after by Mrs. Tansey and the super, as you will be by Aunt Eugenia and Uncle Bruce." Mrs. Hollings was cleaning out the refrigerator, while Gertrude tried to eat her breakfast. In a few hours when she was at school, her parents would be on a plane flying to Greece.

"Remember, Aunt Eugenia is planning a Welcome Gertrude party for you tonight. So go directly to her place after school. She'll be expecting you."

"Can I keep my key?" Gertrude tapped the house key she wore on a silk string around her neck.

"Of course," Mrs. Hollings said. "Though you'll have no use for it till we get home."

She would not take it off for three weeks, she decided. It would remind her that she *had* a home.

Gertrude silently watched the dreary assortment of leftover foods her mother was taking from the refrigerator and tossing into a plastic garbage bag. She felt she was being discarded as well.

"What is it, darling?" Mrs. Hollings's eyes seemed to well up with sympathy.

"Albert is so perfect," Gertrude said.

"Oh Gertrude," Mrs. Hollings sighed. "You'll grow up and find out as I did that there's more to being smart and perfect than being the first in your class to read and write and add a lot of numbers."

Gertrude put her chin on her arms and prepared herself for her mother's "words of encouragement," which she never listened to or believed.

"I couldn't even read till the third grade," Mrs. Hollings said. "I was so mortified, I didn't want to go to school anymore. They called me Dopy Dora. But then it happened. I began to do it, and I worked very hard and got better and better at it. I loved to read. Maybe I loved it more because it had been so difficult for me and I never took it for granted. The thing is to work and to keep trying." Mrs. Hollings paused while Gertrude guessed her next words: "Albert Einstein, Winston

Churchill, Woodrow Wilson had the same problem. We're in good company, Gertie."

"I can't learn my lines for Tituba. Everybody laughs at me." Gertrude pulled the subject back to herself.

"You have to keep going over them, Gertrude, until you have them stamped on your mind and then the actress in you will come out."

"What actress?"

"The one I hear in your room." Her mother smiled. "The one who can mimic six different voices for one story and keep every one of them straight. You have a gift, Gertie. I don't know how you do it."

A gift? What a joke. Her mother who was so smart and quick and successful could not possibly know what it was like to be Gertrude Hollings. She felt she had about as much "gift" as the chicken gizzards her mother had just tossed into the garbage can.

After school, Gertrude mournfully climbed off the bus blocks short of her own stop and made her way with lowered head and hunched shoulders against a howling wind to the river-facing building where the Nugents lived. She hated the wind that blew off the Hudson. It hurt her face and stung her eyes. She hated the huge marble lobby and the buzzer that you had to press before a door opened automatically. *Her* building had Pete or Jerry at the door with a smile or a greeting. "Hey, there's our Gertie," they would call when they saw her coming.

Waiting for the self-service elevator, Gertrude blew on her frozen fingers and looked up at the high ornamented ceiling, just like a castle.

"Where are we, Oliver?" she said in Olivia's voice. "Where have they brought us? Is this a prison?"

An elderly doorman Gertrude had not noticed roused himself from one of the deep lobby benches and shuffled toward her. "You lookin' for somebody, miss?" He seemed alarmed.

"My aunt and uncle," Gertrude said quickly. "Nugent."

He turned his head this way and that, peering near-sightedly. "Where's your friend?"

"My friend?"

"You was talking to someone."

The elevator door opened. Gertrude got in quickly. "I don't understand," she said, but she was afraid this was a bad beginning.

On the Nugents' front door there was a large bright sign in multicolored magic marker. It read, "WELCOME GERTRUDE."

Aunt Eugenia opened the door with a whoop of delight. "We want you to feel as if you are in your own home while you are staying with us." She led Gertrude down the gold carpeted hall that separated the living room from the bedrooms. "I've fixed the room up for you, but please add your personal touches."

The room was the tidiest Gertrude had ever seen. It looked like one of the model bedrooms on the furniture floor of a department store. The bed, covered by a corn-flower sprigged quilt, had matching sheets, pillow covers, and dust ruffle. There were three framed pictures of cornflowers on the wall and in the little vase on the bedside table were cornflowers made of silk. A theme. On the white desk was a blotter, a flowered box of sharpened pencils, and a tensor lamp. The bedside table held another lamp and a box of Kleenex (blue to match the cornflowers). Into the small painted bureau, Aunt Eugenia had already unpacked Gertrude's clothes. They lay in even heaps, each topped by a pomander ball tied up with ribbons and smelling of cloves and lemons. The closet contained another "potpourri," as Eugenie called it. "Lovely smells make such a difference. I took the liberty of unpacking your things and putting them away," she apologized. "I can't keep myself from organizing." On the back of the closet door was a printed list. "Did I make my bed? Did I comb my hair? Did I tidy my desk? Did I put my used clothes in the hamper? Did I brush my teeth?" Next to each question there was a box where a check could be made.

Eugenia pointed out the small bookshelf next to the bathroom door. "Here are some of the books I've picked out that I thought might interest you. If you don't find what you want, tell me or just look around for what you like. Albert is such a reader." Gertrude followed Eugenia into the bathroom which separated her room from Albert's. "Your wash towels and washcloths are blue, Albert's are red. It makes it simpler to coordinate the colors." On the wall beside the sink there was a chart: "How to Get the Most out of Brushing Your Teeth." There were illustrations showing how to move the brush and another checklist. "Did you wash your neck? Did you scrub your nails? Did you . . . take your bath?" Eugenia opened the door into Albert's room. "You see, you're right next door," she said happily. "After you've washed up and settled in, come to the kitchen. I've baked fudge cookies. You have a little time before you go to your tutor, and Albert always likes a snack to get him through his horn lesson. He's due any minute." She clasped her hands on her chest gleefully. "We'll make a little party."

When Eugenia had left, Gertrude washed her hands slowly, staring through the open door into Albert's room. She decided to have a look. Albert's room had a theme, too. The theme was awards. His awards were framed in clear plastic and lined up in a row over his desk. On some of them were gold circles that said FIRST or BEST. There were new ones and old ones. The old ones had stars instead of circles on them and said GOOD WORK or A+. He got these for spelling and math competitions. She went to look at his book shelf: *Know Your Body, Know Your Teeth, So You're Going on a Plane, So You're Going on a Train, So You're Going to the Hospital, So You're Going to Camp, So You're Going to the Dentist, How to Get the Most out of Your Playground, How to Take the ERB, How to Run, How to Be a Winner.* On his bedside table, under a lamp that was shaped like a baseball mitt, were two new books: *So You're Going to Have a Brother or Sister* and *How to Make Baby Your New Friend*.

Gertrude backed out of Albert's room on tiptoe. On her own shelf she found *Frankie, The Story of a Girl Who Lives with Her Aunt and Uncle for One Exciting Year*.

ONE YEAR!? She picked up the book and sank to the floor. Her knees were weak. The front door slammed.

"Am I first?" Albert shouted.

"No, precious. Gertrude got here a few seconds before you did."

Something crashed on the floor. "I wanted to be first. I ran for the stupid bus."

"You wanted to greet her?" Eugenia said hopefully.

"I wanted a few minutes of peace and quiet before the invader from outer space."

"Shhhhhh, Albert, blg nmnmbs sptsss." Gertrude couldn't make out the words, but they were followed by muffled chokings as if a hand had been placed over Albert's mouth.

"Gertrude?" Aunt Eugenia trilled. "Albert's here. He's so eager to see you."

When Gertrude entered the kitchen, Albert did not look up. He sat hunched over his glass of milk. Behind him hung a large bulletin board. Across the top of it in red letters were the words *Albert's Exam Papers* and *Albert's Calendar of Events*.

"Are my parents going to be away for a year or for three weeks?" Gertrude asked.

"A year?" Eugenia looked horrified. Then she noticed the book Gertrude was holding. "Oh, I see." She smiled. "It's because of that book. I thought you'd enjoy the story, dear. It isn't supposed to be your exact experience."

Albert put his milk glass down and began to bang his forehead and laugh in a nasty way. "You thought that because the book said a year your parents would be gone for a year? Oh no."

She felt shame as if it were something heavy on her chest. As she listened to Eugenia apologize and explain the whole misunderstanding, the heaviness got worse and worse. Finally, Eugenia was out of breath. "It's time for you to go to your horn lesson, Albert."

"Is she staying here alone with you while I'm gone?"

"Until she leaves for her tutor."

"Then I'll stay until she goes." Albert folded his arms on his chest and swung his legs back and forth over the linoleum.

"But Albert, what does Gertie's being here have to do with it?"

"She'll eat my cookies. She'll go into my room and touch my things."

"That's silly. We discussed all this thoroughly. You know you told us that you were well prepared for Gertrude's visit and accepted it. We explained to you how Gertie will give you the opportunity to learn what it will be like to share your home as well as your parents with another child. You will have some preparation for your little brother or sister."

All the while Eugenia talked, Albert had been growing more and more agitated. He thumped the table, banged his feet on the chair rung and raked his fingers through his fine straight hair. He looked like a boiler that was building up so much steam it would explode. "I don't want any Dumb Baby. I don't want any Dumb Gertrude. She can hardly read and she writes backwards and can't add numbers and doesn't do script or play cards or Monopoly. She's eleven years old and she has to see a tutor three times a week."

For some reason, watching Albert's outburst made Gertrude feel quite grown up. She knew that Albert was in the throes of an uncontrollable fit of temper and that he would be ashamed of it later. She might even remind him of it and make him suffer for it some time in the future.

Aunt Eugenia, however, was suffering for it right now. Her large eyes appeared as if they were popping with distress. "Albert, I would like to speak with you privately for a moment," she murmured, taking him by the wrist, and more or less yanking him to his feet.

He tried to resist, but her grasp was firm and strong, and she quickly tugged him out of the room. When they were gone, Gertrude helped herself to the remaining cookies on his plate and ate them in a slow deliberate way. She began to study Albert's bulletin board. There were his latest A papers as well as a graph of his grades and his exam schedule. Above the bulletin board was a grouping of photographs. Under each picture was a title written in magic marker. *Albie Builds a Skyscraper* was written beneath a snapshot of Baby Albert playing with his blocks. *Go West, Young Man* was the line under a picture of three-year-old Albert on his tricycle, and *Champ* was beneath a photo of four-year-old Albert in boxing trunks. There was *Albert Plays Ball, Albert on a Pony, Albert Holding the Spelling Bee Prize.*

If the theme of Albert's room was awards, the theme of the Nugents' apartment was Albert: Albert-the-Perfect. Albert-the-Winner. Suddenly Gertrude felt calm and superior. Poor Perfect Prize-Winning Albert. After all these years he was going to get rewarded with a brother or a sister. He, Albert, who who had been such a model child (according to his parents). He, Albert, who had been the center of his parents' lives from the day he was born (according to her parents), was to be rewarded for his perfection with the real "intruder from outer space." Gertrude knew that not all the books of "How to" and "So You're Going to" in the world would help him. Didn't the Nugents know that?

Then, with her mouth full of cookies she realized that they *did* know just that and it was because they knew they had invited her, Gertrude Hollings, to stay with them. She had been invited into their apartment to do a job. She was to teach Albert how to be a brother.

This amazing understanding caused her to rise to her feet, pick up the kitchen telephone, and for the first time in her life dial the number of someone her mother would want to call her "friend."

❧ Six ❧

"JESSIE, guess what I just found out."

"You want an appointment? Let me get my calendar."

"I've been invited here to do an important job."

"What are you talking about?"

"I have to help Albert accept the idea of having a brother or sister."

There was silence while Jessie took this in. "I see," she said slowly. "You're involved in some kind of preparatory work."

"What?"

"Sibling Preparation. It's not a bad idea. A form of family counseling. Your role is to show your client the benefits of being part of a multiple family, of sharing, companionship, and flexibility."

"Exactly," Gertrude said, silently grateful that she herself had been spared the need to deal with any of these things.

"I suppose there's a call for that sort of work," Jessie said grudgingly. "Sibling Preparation." She seemed to be rolling the sound of it around for effect. "You will have to gain your client's respect. Establish rapport or he won't trust you or listen to you." She paused. "Of course, you should have a consultant."

"A what?"

"I suppose I'm the consultant," Jessie answered quickly. "Unless you prefer I be your supervisor."

"Consultant is okay." After she hung up, Gertrude nibbled cookie crumbs from her fingertip and studied the snapshots of Albert on the wall. "You may not like this, Albie," she told them, "but I'm going to prepare you for the most important event of your life. *Albie Gets His Sib.* Hah," she laughed to herself. It was more than a job; it was her mission. Mission Sibling Preparation.

When Albert came back to the kitchen with his mother, his eyes were red and his skin was splotched. He had changed from his school clothes into jeans and a pullover. He was carrying his horn case and his music book. "Sorry if I hurt your feelings just now, Gert," he said, ogling his empty plate.

"Don't worry about it, Albert. It's part of what we all must handle if we are to learn to share and be flexible." She said this in the sort of even voice her tutor Mrs. Crossman used. She wished she had a little treat to offer Albert. She wished she hadn't eaten his cookies. She wished she knew what flexible meant.

It was in a peculiar baby voice that Albert said goodbye.

Gertrude's tutor, Mrs. Crossman, buzzed her up from the lobby and met her at the door to her apartment. As usual, Gertrude was delighted to see there was a little cup of beans on the desk beside the books and games with which they would work. Fifty beans equaled a little gift. The little gift was always a little book. Mrs. Crossman was teaching Gertrude script. They worked slowly and carefully. Gertrude formed the letters using the clues Mrs. Crossman gave her, as well as some of her own. She always checked the birthmark on her right wrist to be sure the letters would go toward it, looping them and linking them so they slanted away from the vaccination mark on her left arm. Though the work went slowly, Gertrude liked to write in script. She thought it was easier than printing. She hated printing. It took so long and her letters always came out scratchy and uneven.

"That's just perfect," Mrs. Crossman said of her page of letters, handing her a bean. "Perhaps try the capitals and keep them nice and high for your last line." At Mrs. Crossman's, Gertrude always felt good about the work she did. She was never given anything she couldn't manage and she always knew Mrs. Crossman would help her to understand what seemed puzzling. She was never embarrassed. Why couldn't school be the same? When Mrs. Crossman had gone over the capitals, she asked to see Gertrude's homework assignment.

"I just remembered. I forgot it," Gertrude said.

"Your mother tells me that your assignments often go through the wash. Why not bring them here, Gertie, and we can look at them together. I could help you so that your school day would go more smoothly."

"Well, I got taken out of the math workbook and put on these sheets," Gertrude complained. "The sheets get all torn up."

"Have you done any of them?"

She looked out the window. "I don't like them. I'm the only one in the class who has sheets."

"Then be sure to bring them next time so you can finish them up. I'll make up a page of problems we can go over in the meantime."

When they had finished the math, Mrs. Crossman took out a board for their game of Uncle Puncle. She placed the dice and plastic cubes on the center of the board. "Do you want red or green?"

"I'll take red." Gertrude picked up the red cube and realized that she was sick of playing Uncle Puncle. "Can't we play chess sometime?" she asked.

Mrs. Crossman smiled. "Chess is a very difficult game, though I'm sure you're fascinated by the shapes of the pieces."

"No, I like to play chess."

Mrs. Crossman raised her brows and continued to smile.

"I play with my father, and sometimes I win."

Gertrude could tell from the way Mrs. Crossman smiled that she did not believe her.

"I like to play chess," she repeated. "Each piece moves in its own way, not like these plastic Uncle Puncles that just go around by the numbers on the dice. The knight goes up and over, and the bishop is very sly, he slides always crosswise."

"Uh-huh. That's so interesting, Gertrude."

Gertrude looked away. She gazed at the beans in the glass cup. They came out of a jar of beans which Mrs. Crossman kept on top of her bookshelf. The jar had a label. "Brookwood Black Beans," it said. There was a picture of a black bean and a list of the nutritional value and contents under the computer code. Every bean was exactly alike. Why was it that fresh beans in the store were so different one from the other, but once they were packaged and labeled they were all the same?

"What are you thinking about?" Mrs. Crossman asked.

"I'm thinking about the beans," Gertrude said. "Just because they're packaged and labeled everybody expects them to be exactly alike."

"Yes, I suppose that's true."

"But when you see fresh beans at the vegetable store you know that some are fat and some are empty and some are sweeter."

"Yes?" Mrs. Crossman's eyes were wide with her effort to follow what Gertrude was trying to say. "What are you trying to say?"

"Nothing." Gertrude shook the dice and threw them. How could she explain that once you got processed and labeled Learning Disabled even the people who thought they knew all about it decided beforehand what to expect of you.

They played Uncle Puncle, and Gertrude won six beans. Mrs. Crossman gave her a lump of stale chocolate and it was time to go.

When she returned to the Nugents, she noticed a few changes. The big sign on the front door now read, "Welcome Gertrude and Albert." There were balloons on it. Gertrude went into her room. The two bathroom doors were open. Albert must have done that. She could see him bent over his desk under his awards with the finger of one hand pressed into the page of a book. The other hand guided a pencil, scratch, scratch. She washed her face in the bathroom, careful not to close the door. He didn't look up. Then she sat on her bed and opened her bookbag. She took out a Mounds candy wrapper, a few loose bread sticks and a broken barrette with plastic hearts on it. As usual, there were no books in her bookbag. She remembered a few math sheets she had crumpled into the pocket of her shirt. She could have done them with her tutor, but it was too late now. She threw them into the wastebasket. It would be mortifying to have them go through Aunt Eugenia's wash. She could just imagine how Albert would react to finding bits of her fractions stuck to his shirts. Sitting at her white desk, Gertrude wished she had a book to open so that she could work the way Albert did, busy and important and Not To Be Disturbed. She had left the social studies book in school. She gazed over her desk out the window across the building's courtyard to a small view of the river.

She was Olivia. The evil impresario Boris Plink had captured her. She was locked in an iron cage in preparation for her debut at Madison Square Garden.

"You will fly through three burning hoops," Boris Plink snarled.

"I cannot. I will singe my feathers and fall."

"You will go through those hoops if I have to shoot you from a cannon. We've sold out the Garden."

"I can't. I won't. Oliver will save me."

"Oliver, hah! I've caught him, too. He is in a cage at this very moment. I am transporting him here. I will teach him to do a high dive into a basin of water."

There was a tenuous tap on the door. "Gertrude, dear, are you all right?" Eugenia opened the door and peered in. "Uncle Bruce is home. It's time for dinner." She looked suspiciously about the room. "Were you singing?"

"I was rehearsing my part for the play." Gertrude picked up her notebook and flipped the pages of it.

When she took her place at the table, Gertrude noticed a neat stack of books piled beside her uncle's setting. At her aunt's place there was an oak tag card which looked like a menu. Eugenia held it up. "Every night at dinner we have discussions," Eugenia explained to Gertrude. "This is our program for tonight's talk." Gertrude read the card: "(1) Greece; (2) What Did I Do Today?; (3) Review." It was no menu.

"The theme of tonight's discussion is Greece." Eugenia took up the platter in front of her plate upon which there were things that looked very much like green cigars.

"These are not green cigars," Eugenia said, giving Gertrude the uncomfortable feeling that her aunt could read minds. "They are called 'dolma' and are a typical Greek dish made of grape leaves stuffed with onions, garlic, rice, nuts, and dill. Our entire dinner tonight will have a Greek theme. This is the sort of food that your parents will be eating for the next few weeks in Athens, Gertie." She began to place a few oily little cigars on each of their plates.

"I'll bet Dora and Charles are taking their first walk around the city." Bruce looked at his watch. "I wouldn't be surprised if they made a beeline to the Acropolis for a little sightseeing before their work begins."

"Do either of you children know what the Acropolis is?" Eugenia smiled innocently. "Gertrude? Albert?"

Gertrude felt her stomach clench.

Albert bobbed excitedly up and down in his seat. "I do! I do!"

"Gertrude?"

She shook her head slowly from side to side as everything within her seemed to sink a little.

"Albert, would you like to talk about the Acropolis?"

Would he ever.

"The Acropolis is a sort of a hill where the ancient Greeks built this beautiful temple to the gods."

"Do you know what the temple was called?" Bruce interrupted.

"The ummmm . . . the Parthenon, and it was for the goddess Athena, who was goddess of wisdom, even though she was only a dumb girl."

Gertrude's sinking feeling went into a nose dive.

"That remark was not necessary," Uncle Bruce said.

"We girls object." Eugenia winked at Gertrude. As she served the veal shanks, Greek style, she gave a short talk on the architecture of Ancient Greece. "The Parthenon is considered one of the world's most perfect buildings." She held up a picture of the building as it might have looked at the time it was built. "Isn't this fun?" she said. "Every night at dinner we will cover another subject. Tonight in honor of your mother and father, Gertrude, it was Greece. In this way we have kept in touch with Dora and Charles and learned heaps of fascinating new things. Tomorrow we'll talk about the myths and legends of the ancient Greeks."

For dessert, Eugenia gave them each a sticky-looking shredded wheat that was drenched in honey and covered with nuts ("It's called baclava").

"With dessert we have our final discussion and Albert knows what that is."

"What did I do today?" Albert piped brightly.

Eugenia nodded. "What *did* you do today?"

"What did I do today?" Albert repeated the question again. "I got A on my history paper and I won the spelling bee. Mrs. Jones says I can move into Book Two for the Young Horn Player."

"What nice news." Bruce nodded happily. "We'll have to post that A paper on the bulletin board."

Eugenia leaned toward Gertrude. "Now it's Gertie's turn."

"I called my friend Jessie," Gertrude said, lingering over the word *friend*. "I went to my tutor, Mrs. Crossman. We worked on script. I got seven beans." Her voice petered out.

Eugenia and Bruce looked at her in an encouraging way that made her feel pathetic. She realized that she hadn't gotten an A or won a spelling bee or been moved into a more advanced horn book. How could she tell them that though she had nothing to pin on the bulletin board she had a plan for Albert and a plan for them all which made Albert's achievements of the day look like peanuts. It was the biggest endeavor of her life and if she succeeded she'd have done something that neither Eugenia nor Bruce had been able to accomplish: Sibling Preparation.

❧ Seven ❧

"Mrs. Tausig," Gertrude said, "I have to know all about the Greek legends, and the Acropolis and the Parthenon and the gods and goddesses, especially Athena."

Mrs. Tausig, the librarian, showed her where the books were on mythology. "These should keep you busy, Gertrude." She took a volume from the shelf and opened it. "Though they aren't on your usual level and there are very few pictures."

Gertrude snatched the book from her hand. "I don't have to have pictures to understand what I'm reading." She was aware of Mrs. Tausig's gaze following her to the corner table near the wall where she spread the books before her. The sunlight that flooded through the window made her feel as if she were safe at the center of a yellow bubble. If she was going to win Albert's respect and accomplish her mission, she had to do it at the dinner table and it looked like the subject would have to be the myths of the ancient Greeks. She opened the book on mythology and began to read. It was very difficult.

There was a god, and his name was Zeus. How would you say such a word? Usually when she came to words like that she wanted to close the book, but she couldn't do that now. She had to prepare herself for Dinner Discussion. This god named Z . . . had a daughter, Athena. Gertrude said the word out loud, slowly. She remembered Albert had mentioned Athena. Athena had been born full-grown from her father's forehead, dressed in full armor. Gertrude had to look up for a moment just to imagine such a thing. It was so amazing that she read the sentence again, to get the picture of it in her mind. Athena was her father's favorite child, the only one he entrusted with his most devastating weapon, the thunderbolt. Gertrude turned the page. She didn't want to stop reading. Athena was the embodiment of wisdom, reason, and purity. Athens was her special city, the olive her special tree, and the owl her special bird. The owl? If she were alone Gertrude would have preened and blinked like Olivia. When she had finished reading the section on the Greek gods, she decided to brush up on the Parthenon, just in case it came up in conversation at the dinner table again. She rummaged among the books Mrs. Tausig had given her. It was hard to know what to tackle first.

Jessie marched into the library with Nina behind her. Though Gertrude tried to screen herself behind a book, she plunked down beside her. "What are you doing, Gert?"

"Research."

"For your role as Tituba?"

"For my job at the Nugents."

Nina leaned over the library table and picked up the top book. "*Myths and Legends of Ancient Greece*. Are you going into the travel business, Jessie?"

"Those are Gertie's books."

"My mother is still furious over what you did with my hair."

"I'm not in the beauty parlor business anymore. I just needed more practice and nobody would let me work on them except for you and Aggie."

"Aggie had to wear a hat for two weeks," Nina recalled. "How's the tutoring going?"

Jessie glared at Gertrude. "Same problem. I need practice and I can't get clients."

"I'd let you." Nina nibbled on her fingernail. "But I see my regular tutor twice a week."

Gertrude was amazed that she said it, just like that. Why, she wasn't even embarrassed.

"I could fit you in," Jessie said excitedly. "I'd do your hair again, too."

"I'll think about it." Nina looked up at the library clock. "It's time to go to drama."

In drama, Mrs. Daniels said, "Gertrude, do you still need to read from your script?"

Gertrude looked around her and realized that no one else was holding a script. Had they all memorized their lines? "My part is very long."

"I know, dear. Perhaps someone at home can help you go over it."

Before Gertrude could answer, a familiar voice piped up. "I can help her with her lines. I'm very good at that."

"Yes, Jessie."

"You see, she has a special problem. It's not just the memorizing. It has to do with . . ."

"Not now," Mrs. Daniels interrupted. "It's up to Gertrude, Jess."

The narrator began to speak.

Gertrude began to worry. She had gone over her lines with her mother. She knew she could say the words straight this time. But she hadn't thought of memorizing them.

The narrator had stopped his speech and he was looking at her. She was so worried that she hadn't been listening to him. He repeated her cue. When she read, every word was right, but why were they giggling?

Mrs. Daniels said, "Could you try not to holler, Gertie. Give the words some meaning, if you can. Take it again, dear."

"I-am-Tituba-from-the-sun-warmed-island-of-Barba-dos-where-my-mistress-sold-me-with-my-husband-John-Indian-to-the Reverend-Parris-of-Boston-in-the-Bay-Col-ony," Gertrude said in a rush without drawing breath.

When she finished, the giggles had turned to laughter. Gertrude rolled her eyes, sucked in her cheeks, made her mouth like a circle and blinked. This was her fish-face. She had practiced it often. Now they were laughing at her and she was part of the joke.

"Gertrude," Mrs. Daniels said sternly, "if you want to get silly and disruptive, you can do so in some other place and at some other time."

"She sounds like a train conductor," Myron Franks pointed out. "Boston, Barbados, Bermuda, The Bronnnnnx."

"That's enough, Myron," Mrs. Daniels interrupted. "Let's get on with the scene."

The next time her lines came up, Gertrude read them in a flat whisper. She got the words right, but they made no sense to her. Mrs. Daniels did not ask her to "take it again." No one laughed. They just seemed impatient for her to be done.

As soon as drama was over, Jessie cornered her. "You look like Linus with his security blanket, holding on to that script. You better come home with me for a session."

This was not an invitation; it was an order.

Jessie lived halfway between the Hollingses and the Nugents. There were two beds in the room she shared with her half sister Victoria, who lived with the Bogueses every weekend. "Victoria is fun to watch," Jessie said. "She's sixteen and she wears tons of makeup and wants to be a model. Her mother wants her to be a lawyer. They fight about it a lot. She tells me things, and I try to counsel her."

"You what?"

"I give her advice. She respects my analyses of her problems."

"Where's your brother?" Gertrude remembered Jessie's other client.

"At his tutor's." Jessie looked sour. "Let's eat something."

In the kitchen she came up with broken oatmeal pecan cookies and poured out apple juice. "Don't eat too much. It might interfere with your concentration." She unfolded her copy of the script on the table. "Okay, I'll read the last line of the speech before yours."

"Can't I finish my juice?"

"If I can chew and talk, so can you."

"I need to see the script for the first word."

"I'll tell it to you." Though Jessie had a small role as the Reverend Parris' sick wife, she had learned most of the other parts by heart.

"But I need to hold the pages, even if I don't look at them."

"*I'll* hold the pages; you can hold this." Jessie gave her a folded paper napkin.

"I just have to see the first line."

Jessie banged her fist on the table. "You start off saying who you are. What's so hard about that? Who are you?"

"I am Tituba," Gertrude began quickly. "From the sun-warmed island of Barbados where my mistress sold me with my husband John Indian." It was like learning to pedal a two-wheeler. She could do it. She was doing it, and in her hand was a paper napkin.

When she had finished, Jessie said, "Now you have to go through it four more times till it's smooth."

"Smooth?"

They ran through the script four times more and then Jessie said they could stop. "You even said your lines with feeling that time. You sounded like an actress."

"Thanks." Gertrude glowed.

Jessie seemed to be waiting for something. "What do you say to me?"

"Oh Jessie," Gertrude realized, "you coached me like a . . . a . . ."

"A professional acting coach."

"Yes."

"Remember some of my techniques, Gertrude. You can use them with your cousin. You will get nowhere without respect and rapport."

When she returned to the apartment, Albert was already doing his homework. Gertrude arranged her books on her desk. She hoped he would come in and see them. The scratch-scratch of his pencil continued without let-up until Aunt Eugenia's voice called, "Albert, it's 4:30 horn practice time." Within minutes the bleat of the horn took up where the scratch of the pencil had let off. What next? Gertrude wondered. No sooner did she wonder this than "Time to set the table" was trilled into her room. She couldn't believe it. Albert Nugent's every minute was accounted for.

At the dinner table Uncle Bruce unfolded his napkin and began the Dinner Discussion. "What did you do today, Gertrude?"

"I went home with my friend Jessie Bogues and she coached me in my role of Tituba for our play in drama."

"Who was Tituba?"

"Tituba was a slave from Barbados who was accused of being a witch in colonial times."

"Gertrude the witch. Where's your broomstick?" Albert cracked.

"I am not a witch," Gertrude corrected. "I *act* a witch."

"Acting is dumb. It's dumb standing around pretending to be somebody else. We don't have acting in my school. Acting is for kids who go to Bradwin and can't learn to read books."

"Albert," Eugenia scolded, "what a thing to say."

"But it's true," Albert insisted. "*You* said so. You told me nobody learns anything at those progressive schools except how to goof off."

"I don't think I said that exactly." Eugenia was the color of a stoplight. "I'm sure Gertie learns heaps of fabulous things."

"I learned a story today," Gertrude said quickly. She

had at least to gain Albert's attention if not his rapport and respect. "It's a good story and it's Greek." She looked at her aunt for encouragement. "Isn't this myths-of-ancient-Greece night?"

"We thought we would do architecture first," said Eugenia, but Gertrude had begun her story.

"There was a girl named Arachne who bragged and bragged that she could weave as well as the goddess Athena." Gertrude kept her eyes on Albert. "This made Athena so mad that she disguised herself as an old woman to trick Arachne into making the boast to her face. When the trick worked, Athena threw off her disguise and said, 'Okay, prove your boast.' She set up two looms next to each other and they both began to weave."

"Is this a very long story, Gertie dear?" Bruce said. They were all eating their soup. Gertrude had not touched hers.

"Then when Athena saw how good Arachne was, she got furious and ripped the cloth right off her loom and tore it up. Arachne got so scared she tried to kill herself."

"Sweetheart, your soup." Eugenia tapped the side of her bowl.

"And then what happened?" Albert leaned toward Gertrude on both elbows, his eyes like blue pools.

"Athena took pity on Arachne and changed her into a spider. To this day she weaves her wonderful webs." Gertrude bent to slurp some spoonfuls before Eugenia collected her plate.

"That was a nice story, Gertie, but it's hard to eat and conduct a monologue at the same time," Bruce said.

"We don't want you to starve while you're with us." Eugenia laughed. "Dinner Discussion should be open to all of us. It should not be a solo performance."

"Perhaps Albert would like to tell us something about the Parthenon." Bruce looked encouragingly at his son.

"Oh, the Parthenon," Gertrude said as her cousin drew breath. "It's a terrible shame about the way they stripped it. My parents could have seen as much if they'd gone to the British Museum. What would the goddess Athena have thought? She was not only fierce and ruthless," leaning toward Albert, "but defender of the state."

"Speaking of the state," Uncle Bruce said, "Albert will now tell us something about the city-states of the ancient Greeks while Gertrude eats her dinner."

As Albert droned on, Gertrude ate with pleasure. Her cousin had neither taunted nor teased her from the moment she began to speak. In fact, she had caught his intent gaze riveted upon her. It dawned on Gertrude that he looked exactly as he had years before, when sitting on the floor of her bedroom pleading for another Owl Game. "Tell me one, Gertie," he would say.

"Make one up for yourself, Albert," she would answer.

"I can't. I don't know how."

She *did* know how. Was this the way she could gain his respect and rapport?

❧ Eight ❧

I T was the hour after dinner when they were supposed to be doing their homework. Gertrude had settled on her pretty bed with the story of the Trojan War, when she became aware of Albert leaning on the bathroom door.

"That story about Athena turning Arachne into a spider, where did you get it?"

"It's in my mythology book," she said grudgingly. She didn't want him to read the myths and catch up.

"Can I borrow it?"

"I'm reading it now, and you haven't finished your homework."

"It's not fair." He folded his arms on his chest. "You never get any homework at that dummy school you go to, so you can sit around all day reading fairy tales and pretending to be a witch."

She glared and pursed her lips together and took a deep breath as if she were about to make a devastating retort. However, none came to mind.

He took a step toward her. "It's not fair. You make people think you're stupid and they don't bother you."

"I'm not stupid," Gertrude corrected in a high-handed voice. "I'm Learning Disabled. I got labeled Learning Disabled."

"Dumb," he snarled, backing out of her room and closing the door behind him. "Dumb, dumb, dumb," she heard him repeat loudly as he went back into his own room. "Dumb, dumb."

She stormed to the door and flung it open. "Learning disabled, learning disabled, learning disabled. L.D. is not dumb."

"Prove it."

"L.D. is if six looks like nine and twenty-one like twelve and the letters . . . the letters . . ." She was running out of breath. ". . . go every way and left and right get mixed up so you can't play games right and . . ."

"How come you beat me at chess?"

"Because I *like* chess and figured it out!"

He narrowed his eyes to slits. "I don't believe you, and you don't work."

"It takes longer for me to learn things than other people, even though I am very bright," Gertrude quoted her mother. "Albert Einstein, Winston Churchill, Woodrow Wilson were like me."

"Like you?" He believed her less than she believed her mother. "You sit around reading fairy tales and you're so mean you won't let me borrow them and I study two hours a night and I'm a whole year younger than you are." His round face went soft with self-pity. "I don't ever get a chance to read fairy tales."

Gertrude shrugged. "All right, Albert." She picked up the book of myths. "Here. I suppose I could let you have them. They're just the baby myths. The others would be too strong for you. But you can handle these."

"What others?"

"The ones in my other book." She turned away and bit her lip, as if she had said too much. "I can't talk about it."

"What other book?"

She stared at him for a long moment, and then drew closer. "It's secret. I can't tell you." Her voice became a whisper.

"You have to." Albert grew pale. "What secret book?"

Gertrude had been making up the script as she went along. It was just like an Owl Game. "Since it's a secret, I can't tell you."

"Where is it? What's in it?"

"The myths in my secret book are different, because they aren't myths at all." She darted him a quick glance. She was taking a real risk now. Would Albert buy her story? "They are real."

"I don't believe you."

"I knew you wouldn't. You're too young to handle this." She offered him the open book. "Take these. They can do you no harm."

He accepted the book and she closed the door behind him.

On the back of the closed door was a full-length mirror. Gertrude was gripped by her reflection in it. Her long body, her long neck, her bright round dark owly eyes and halo of frizzy blond hair that could never stay in an elastic or a barrette for more than five minutes — all combined to make her appear different. She lifted her arms as if they were wings and raised her brows. She was Athena. In one fist she held the great thunderbolt. She felt its power surge through her. With the surge of power driving her she opened the door to Albert's room, her arm aloft and stood majestically before him. He looked up from his book.

"What's up, Gertie?"

"I have a secret to impart, Albert."

"Why are you standing like that? Why is your arm up like that?" He looked alarmed.

"I have held the mighty bolt, Albert. I have touched its power."

"The what?"

"The power has gone through my hand." She made her face stony and her eyes staring.

"Oh boy." Albert tried to laugh. "Big deal. Gertie and the magic thunderbolt. What did you do with it? Put it in the hamper?"

She waved vaguely toward the bathroom and pointed to the tub behind her. "It is there. Do not mock, or the gods will seek vengeance."

"Oh boy." Albert picked up his book. "You really are something."

"Albert, do not mock," Gertrude said gravely. She turned and glided out the door. Albert's eyes followed her. She could see them in the mirror. They were round and quizzical. She had enjoyed herself, but maybe she had gone too far. He was curious, but he hadn't believed the act. How gullible was he? He obviously had loved her story at dinner and wanted to hear more, had almost believed she had a secret book, but then she had lost him with the thunderbolt. She had gone too far, too fast. She would need to be careful.

The next morning Gertrude opened her eyes to the sound of Albert brushing his teeth. She was curious to see if he consulted the chart over the sink on "How to Get the Most out of Brushing."

He did. His eyes squinted and read as he brushed. "Stop staring," he warned and spat a final sudsy mouthful at the drain. "It isn't your turn in here anyway. I go from seven-thirty to seven-forty. It's seven thirty-seven."

"But this is my shower morning."

He looked over his shoulder at the tub. "I thought you put the . . . thunderbolt in there. I thought you said not to go near it."

She couldn't tell if he was teasing or not. Was it possible he had believed her story? "I did put the thunderbolt in there," Gertrude said, "but *I* can use the tub."

"What about me?" His face was very serious.

"I wouldn't try it if I were you."

He turned on his heels and left the bathroom.

Perhaps she hadn't gone too far. But what should she do next? She needed to proceed with care. She needed help. Where should she turn?

"Mrs. Tausig, I want more books about the gods."

"I thought you got them yesterday."

"I need to find out how they were worshiped. I need details."

"You probably need the encyclopedia." She frowned. "I hope it isn't too hard for you." Mrs. Tausig pulled the thick G volume of the encyclopedia from the shelf. "The type is small, Gertie, and there aren't many pictures."

"I promise I won't get frustrated."

Mrs. Tausig laughed as she handed her the book.

"*There* you are." Jessie came rushing in. "I have some time to review the math with you."

"I'm doing S.P. work," Gertie said huffily. "Not now."

Jessie followed her to a table and watched while she opened to Greece. "That's too difficult for you, Hollings. You'll need help."

Gertrude didn't answer. The type was small, and there were very few pictures. She began to use her fingers to guide her along.

"Why are you moving your mouth?" Jessie said.

"What's this word?" Gertrude pushed the book toward her.

"Oracle." Jessie smiled with satisfaction. "I better pitch in." She pulled her chair closer. "Let's call this a tutorial. I'll read a paragraph and then you read a paragraph."

In this way they read that only the priests were allowed inside the temples. Ordinary people worshiped out-of-doors. Sometimes they consulted oracles. Oracles were priestesses of the gods. Apollo had a famous oracle at Delphi. The oracles could go into a swoon and make predictions about the future. The predictions were usually vague enough to turn out right. The oracles drew crowds from all over Greece.

"That was very good," Jessie complimented after Gertrude's paragraph. "I'll have you zipping through it yourself in no time. My mother says I am a natural-born tutor."

"Maybe you are," Gertrude said.

"You better come to my house for a follow-up session this afternoon. We need to go over your part for the play."

"I have to see my real tutor."

"I'm not real?!"

"I mean my other tutor. But Jessie, I need to know what the oracles looked like."

"I can't help you with that," Jessie said simply. "Why don't you go to the museum? They've got a lot of rooms full of old Greek stuff."

"How do you know so much?"

"It's part of my job." Jessie opened her notebook and took out her famous calendar. It was a tiny booklet with the days of each month marked off in a separate square. "Another part of my job is to get some sense of my client's home environment."

"I'm not living at home."

"That doesn't matter. I need to acquaint myself with the dynamics of the setting in which you live. My mother thinks it is crucial to establishing an effective working relationship."

"But I never . . . I don't invite." Gertrude's heart sank. One of her primary rules would be broken. The home Gertrude and the school Gertrude would meet. She couldn't even imagine it. "I'll ask my aunt," she said weakly.

"Tell her I'm free tomorrow at four," Jessie concluded crisply and closed her calendar.

❧ *Nine* ❧

O<small>N</small> the way to her tutor's, Gertrude decided that instead of stopping for her usual cup of cocoa at a luncheonette, she would get off the crosstown bus one stop sooner at Fifth Avenue so that she could visit the Metropolitan Museum.

A guard directed her to the Greek collection. She walked quickly through the immense lobby, past the museum shop, past a planting of orchids surrounded by benches upon which people sat waiting and resting, through a gallery and into a high, arched, pink marble corridor, flanked by ancient sculpture. Even the light that filtered down from the openwork of the ceiling was pink. It cast a soft glow on the stone figures as well as the living ones who stood or strolled from one end of the gallery to the other. For a moment Gertrude felt lost and wondered why she had come. She would be late. As she turned to leave, she noticed a stone box in the shape of a man lying on his back. The curly marble hair framed a cheerful blank-eyed face. Its expression was peaceful and sweet. MARBLE SARCOPHAGUS. EARLY IVTH CENTURY B.C. FROM KITION, the label on him read. So it was a coffin. A man's body had lain within the stone. The body of an ancient Greek who had lived in the fourth century before Christ was born. As she regarded the stone face, so passive and still, the room grew distant. The high arched ceiling, the pink light, the bustle of schoolchildren and the murmur of the crowd withdrew. Time fell away as well. Thousands of years ago Athena held the thunderbolt, Greeks worshiped out-of-doors, the Parthenon blazed with light, oracles foretold the future, and a dead man had been placed within this very marble coffin. She could touch the stone. She could practically touch the past.

"Do you think the guy is still in there?" a small boy who was part of a group of schoolchildren asked Gertrude.

"In a way," she said, buttoning her jacket. It was time to leave.

Coming out of the museum into the cloudy raw day, Gertrude saw a line of chilly-looking boys in soccer uniforms with the word *Foxbrite* across their chests. They were being herded into Central Park by a distraught gym teacher. She searched among the faces, looking for Albert. When she found him, she raised her hand to wave, but his piercing stare made her catch her breath and pause with her hand still foolishly in the air.

"Don't you dare wave," was the message she read

in his eyes. She lifted her head, turned on her heels and walked quickly in the direction of her tutor's.

A Droste chocolate apple sat beside the glass of beans on Mrs. Crossman's desk. Her expression was tragic.

"I'm sorry I'm a little late. My bus got stuck," Gertrude lied.

Mrs. Crossman smiled sadly and laced her fingers together on her knees. For an awful moment Gertrude imagined that she was about to say something truly horrible. Something about how she would never learn and could not hope to graduate from high school. She was so nervous imagining disaster that at first she didn't even hear Mrs. Crossman's words.

"I have been offered a full-time job at a school. So you see, Gertie, I will have to give up all my private tutoring. This is very sad news for me."

"Oooh, for me too." Gertrude sighed miserably, catching on just in the nick of time. "I am soooo sorry."

The thought that she might have three whole free afternoons a week was like being given three boxes of Droste apples tied up with ribbon.

"Of course, I wanted to inform your parents first so they could help to prepare you for this news, but they are in Greece. This job came up so suddenly." She wrung her hands a little. "But you will not be stranded."

"Stranded?"

"Mrs. Barnes has promised to take on all my students. She has even arranged to give you the same time slot."

The three gift boxes tied with ribbon dissolved.

"Now then," with a little clap of her hands, "let's have a lovely last session so we don't feel too sad." Mrs. Crossman picked up the chocolate apple. "I've added up all your beans and guess what they come out to?"

"Can I eat it now?"

"It's yours, Gertrude."

Carefully, Gertrude broke off a wedge of chocolate and offered it to Mrs. Crossman.

"Why not? My waistline will wait." She began to nibble. "What have you been doing in school, Gertrude?"

"I've been reading as much as I can about the civilization of ancient Greece."

"Is this a school project?"

"It's a private project. My teacher is allowing me to use the books in the school library."

"What books?"

"Today I read the Encyclopaedia Britannica, Volume G, on Greece. I also read a book on the myths."

Mrs. Crossman stopped chewing. "The encyclopedia is a difficult book for you, Gertie. Didn't you find it frustrating?"

"It was hard," Gertrude nodded, "but my friend Jessie helped me and I got a lot out of it."

"You don't mean the adult Britannica, dear. You mean the Book of Knowledge."

"I mean the Encyclopaedia Britannica. Volume G."

Mrs. Crossman put the uneaten part of her chocolate on a piece of tissue paper and turned abruptly to a note pad on her desk. Under the note pad was a folder which was labeled "Gertrude Hollings." Mrs. Crossman opened the folder and scrutinized the pages within it. From what Gertrude could see, the pages were covered with lists of test scores and notations. For a curious moment she felt as if the real-living-breathing Gertrude Hollings existed only within that folder. If she, like the can of beans, had been processed and labeled, she supposed the test scores must be the ingredients listed on the side of the wrapper next to the computer code. Calories, vitamins, nutritional value, and artificial coloring. The Gertrude Hollings who created Owl Games and undertook Sibling Preparation, the Gertrude Hollings with a long neck and round black-brown eyes seemed to be vanishing while the page of test scores and notations would probably stumble sadly through life. As Mrs. Crossman jotted notes on the page, Gertrude raised her brows and sucked in her cheeks till they met over her tongue. Then she filled her chest with air and made her eyes distant and blank. She was doing the oracle of Delphi. She flared her nostrils and tried to flutter her eyelids as if a swoon was under way and a message from the gods about to issue from her mouth. She wished she had a mirror.

"My gracious, Gertrude, what's wrong with you?" Mrs. Crossman had looked up suddenly.

Gertrude rolled her tongue into her cheek. "It's my tooth."

"Your tooth? You looked as if you were having a fit."

"I'm so sad about you leaving." Gertrude rubbed her cheek and put on her saddest face. "I'll miss you and my tooth hurts."

"I never saw such an expression before," Mrs. Crossman said.

"That's because I was never so sad before," Gertrude lied.

"Don't feel sad. This is a fine piece of progress. I am going to tell your new tutor as well as your school about this development."

"What development?"

"You've made some real strides."

Gertrude was alarmed. What had she done? Would they make her stop reading fairy tales? Would they put her back in the workbook?

Mrs. Crossman was glowing as if she had done something wonderful. "I wish your parents were here so I could tell them of this nice breakthrough."

"Breakthrough?" She felt sick to her stomach. The chocolate taste was suddenly cloying. Mrs. Crossman would talk to the school. The school would talk to her teachers. She would be asked to work. What if she couldn't? She'd be dumb again. Only worse, because this time she had really tried.

❧ *Ten* ❧

S HE was unpacking her knapsack onto the white desk when an Owl Game commenced. Olivia said, "Oliver, what do I do about trying to fly through the burning hoops?"

Oliver's cage had just been placed beside Olivia's in Boris Plink's studio. "We will devise a protective shield for your wings, Olivia," Oliver said.

"But how will I fly with extra weight on my wings?"

"The shield will be as light as feathers."

"What is as light as feathers?"

"Feathers," Oliver said in Gertrude's deep Oliver-voice. "I will make you a shield of feathers."

"Oh, Oliver," Olivia crooned, "you are a genius."

"Stop communicating," Boris Plink warned.

"Gertrude." Albert stood in her doorway. "Who were you talking to?" His eyes darted about the room.

"Huh?"

"It was like a room full of people." He opened her closet and peered into it.

"I was talking to myself," she admitted.

He raised his brows. "I don't believe you. It was magic."

"Why don't you believe me?" She couldn't understand him. Was it that he could not believe what he could not do? Just as she sometimes felt there must be magic in being able to add up a column of numbers quickly or in playing a piece on the piano?

"Did it have to do with the Greeks and the religion?" he whispered. "Or the thunderbolt?"

"The religion? The thunderbolt?" Was he kidding?

"I mean the myths."

"It had to do with a lot of things which I cannot talk about and you shouldn't know about. Now go away." She moved toward him as if to push him out of her room.

He didn't budge. "What were you doing at the museum?"

"That's my business."

"Does it have to do with the religion, I mean the myths?"

"I can't discuss it."

"What's in the museum?"

"Greek things. Ancient and very strong."

They stood within inches of each other. Albert's head was bent toward her. Was he smiling or sneering? "An altar? A statue of the gods?"

She couldn't tell if this was a taunt. She closed her

eyes so that she wouldn't have to watch him. "A coffin," she whispered. "A sarcophagus. I cannot say more."

"You have to. Tell me, Gertie." There was a new urgency in his voice.

When she opened her eyes she saw that his smile was gone and his expression was intense. He meant it! He really wanted to know.

"Tell me, Gertie. Tell me." His face was overtaken by a tic, like a pool of water rippled by wind. His brow furrowed, his nose wrinkled, and his mouth zipped into one cheek.

"What do you want me to tell you?"

"Where do you get your stories from, and your voices and your Gertie Games? Where do you learn that?"

"They come to me." Gertrude was amazed. How could he not know?

"But where do you learn it?"

"You don't learn it. It's inside you. It's *there*."

Eugenia's voice called down the hallway. "Four-thirty, Albie. I don't hear the horn."

He ticked again and looked guiltily over his shoulder. "It's my horn practice time."

"Why did you stare at me like that when you saw me on the steps of the museum?"

"I was warning you not to call to me or wave," he said. "They would have teased me. I hate to be teased."

"So do I," Gertrude said.

"I didn't mean to hurt your feelings. I'm sorry."

Gertrude nodded her acceptance of his apology. "In the museum there is a sarcophagus. His lips are made of marble," she whispered. "But he speaks to me. He is Kition, fourth century B.C."

"He speaks? How?"

Now they were both whispering. "Like an oracle. He gives me power." She widened her eyes. In fact, she felt that she *had* been given powers that day. "I have said too much. You must never tell."

"I swear I'll never tell."

"Swear on the sarcophagus of Kition that you will never tell."

"Alberrrrrt," Eugenia called, "I don't hear your horn."

He blinked, as if the spell had been broken. His expression was skeptical again. "I swear on the sarcophagus of Kition," he said in a singsong way that made it sound like a bit of gibberish. Albert returned to his room and shortly after the awful bleat of his horn could be heard. Gertrude covered her ears and puzzled over what had just happened. Did he really believe her?

When they sat down to dinner, Eugenia held up the program card. "Wednesday." She smiled. "On Wednesday we discuss our weekend plans and then we do a review of current events. Stories in the news."

"I don't want to go to Hillside this weekend," Albert

said. "I want to stay in the city for Josh Mallory's birthday party."

"You can't stay by yourself. You're too young," Eugenia told him. "And it's too late for me to find someone who'll take you."

"Eddie Fringer says I can stay overnight with him so I can go to the party."

"I don't think so." Eugenia and Bruce were looking anxiously at one another. "We've made plans for the weekend in the country and you are part of those plans, Albert."

"Aren't we going to talk about Greece?" Gertrude interrupted.

"Greece?" Eugenia looked alarmed. "We hadn't planned on it. Wednesday is current events night. Is there something you would like to say, Gertrude?"

"I've been reading about the gods and goddesses and how they were worshiped."

"Have you?" Bruce asked grimly.

"Did you know that the only people allowed in those temples were the priests? They conducted out-of-doors ceremonies for the people. The gods and goddesses had oracles. Oracles were often priestesses. They could go into states or swoons and say things that foretold the future."

"I think the proper time for this discussion would be at our bedtime book review, Gertrude dear. We have book review at nine-thirty," Bruce said.

"Gertrude darling," Eugenia giggled, "do you always talk so much at dinner?"

"She talks to herself, too," said Albert. "She talks when she's all alone."

"That's because Gertrude is an imaginative and whimsical girl," Eugenia explained. "She invents voices and stories and it amuses her to pretend things."

"But I didn't pretend about the oracles," Gertrude said. "They are real."

"I've been reading the book of myths you gave me, and I didn't read about them."

"They wouldn't be in the book of myths because they're real."

"How do you know the myths weren't real?"

"Albert, you must be joking." Eugenia laughed uneasily.

But Gertrude guessed that Albert was not joking.

"How was soccer practice?" Bruce changed the subject.

"It wasn't practice. It was a game. We played Givens and won."

"Do you ever play Bradwin?"

"Bradwin?" he crowed. "Do they have a team?"

"We do," Gertrude said.

"Do Learning Disabled kids play games backwards?"

"Albert, where on earth did you get that phrase, learning disabled?" Eugenia looked as if he had used a bad word.

"She told me about it." He pointed a thumb at

Gertrude. "She said it's why she doesn't ever have any work to do."

"Learning disabled children can be helped by new methods and teachers who are specially trained in using them. Children like Gertrude can overcome their problem, uh — disability."

"Children like Gertrude, labeled Learning Disabled." Gertrude's spirits sunk. It sounded as if they were all alike, as if they were beans in a can. How would Albert respect her if he thought she was damaged, disabled? Whatever fancy words you called it, they both knew that Albert had A's where she had "A Problem." He had "good work" where she had "no motivation." He was perfect. She was not.

Immediately after dinner, the evening program set in. First there was Clean-Up and Clear-the-Table. This was followed by Homework, which lasted one and a half hours and Homework Review. Then came one half-hour television show and after that was Bed Preps. Bed Preps started at nine o'clock and included a bath or shower, teeth scrubbing and twice-weekly shampoo. Book Review for Fun lasted fifteen minutes and was concluded with Lights Out.

"Can I use your bathtub?" Albert asked his mother.

"You have a perfectly good one of your own, dear."

"I don't like my tub."

"That's silly."

"I won't use it." He shook his head.

Eugenia shot a quick glance at Gertrude. "Are you shy about sharing it?"

Albert didn't answer.

"You can use my tub for now," his mother said understandingly.

Later when they gathered in Albert's room for Book Review, Eugenia said, "Since Gertie told us about the myths she has been reading for pleasure at dinner last night, why don't you tell us what you're reading for fun, Albert?"

"*How to Make Baby Your Friend* is about a boy named Joey whose mom and dad are expecting a baby. In the end they let him give it a bath," Albert said dismally. "I hated it."

Eugenia stared unhappily at Albert's floor. "Perhaps while Gertie is with us we'll suspend Book Review."

"Could we play checkers?" Albert asked.

Eugenia stood up to leave. "Just one game."

Albert ran to fetch the board. "I want the red."

"You got red last time."

"But I won last time, so I choose."

"Albert the winner," Gertrude scoffed.

"Gertie the loser," he countered, setting up the pieces.

What was this? Another label? Gertrude wondered.

❧ *Eleven* ❧

NINA was about to toss her lunch into the trash can when she turned abruptly. "Do you want it, Gertie?" She held the apple out.

"No thanks."

"Jessie tells me she's going to make a house call at your place this afternoon. She says you're turning into her big success."

"I don't know about that."

"Let me tell you, I was her big failure. My mother said after what she did to my hair, I shouldn't let her in the house." Nina sat down. "But I like Jessie. She has a lot of . . . I don't know . . ."

"Confidence?" Gertrude suggested.

"She's very determined, too. She leaned toward Gertrude. "You don't remember me, but I was at Partridge Mellon. I stayed until second grade."

"You did?"

Nina nodded miserably. "I used to see you in assembly, but you didn't see me because you never looked up."

"Why did you leave?"

"Nobody would eat with me. They said my lunchbox was contaminated and my hair had cooties and I couldn't do my work." She reflected on these things. "Mrs. Brossard always said to me, 'Now you just sit there, Nina Godwin, until you finish the whole page.' I sat there for three hours. I never did do a whole page. I didn't want to." She smiled to herself. "Actually, I didn't know how to. It's better here. They don't tease a lot and Jessie isn't bad. It's just that she wants to be all grown up with a career."

Gertrude had an idea. "Should we tutor her in being a kid?"

Nina laughed. "How to Be Silly. How to Not Pay Attention."

"How to Lose Your Homework."

"Can I come visit your aunt's house with Jessie this afternoon?"

Gertrude was so taken aback by the question that she couldn't think of a way to say no.

Jessie gasped as Gertrude opened the door into the Nugents' foyer. "It's like a church." She pointed to the large framed photographs of Albert which were hung under lights on the dark walls. Unlike the snapshots in the kitchen, these were formal studio portraits of her cousin, taken every other year of his life and hung in sequence. Albert at two, four, six, and eight sat in the same chair. The effect of the portraits was like an

advertisement for bread which showed a child miracu-
lously "shoot up" several feet in a flash because of the
vitamin-enriched food he had eaten.

"Come see his head," Nina called from the living
room which she had hurried into. Jessie did not com-
ment on the small sculpted bust of Albert or the water-
color of him hung over the sofa. However, when they
walked into the kitchen, she gave her verdict, "A classic
anal compulsive household. I never saw such a neat
kitchen. Do they keep food in it?"

"Take a look at that bulletin board," Nina crowed.

Jessie whistled and began to read out loud from
Albert's papers. "A-plus, excellent work. Albert's test
scores graph."

"Wait till you see the stuff hanging in the bathroom,"
Gertrude said. What would Jessie have to say about
"How to Get the Most out of Brushing Your Teeth"?

"Where is everybody?" Nina looked around worriedly. "Can they hear us?"

"My aunt teaches a class today, and Albert's at soccer
practice."

She poured out glasses of milk and found some of
Eugenia's fudge brownies. They sat down to eat.

"Too bad they aren't around." Jessie looked disappointed. "I would like to have observed the family
dynamics. It helps in my work."

"Have another cookie." Nina winked at Gertrude.
"I'll bet that helps in your work, too."

Jessie opened her knapsack and took out the script

for Tituba. "This is not a social visit, Nina," she said primly. "I'm here to give Gertrude a coaching session."

"I won't bother you," Nina assured her.

Jessie smoothed the script on the table. "We'll run through it three times and then I'll review your math homework. I did not come over here to play Parcheesi."

As Gertrude began to recite her lines, Nina leaned toward her, cupping her narrow chin in the palm of one hand and listening as if her eyes could hear as well as her ears.

"I am Tituba, from the sun-warmed island of Barbados where my mistress sold me with my husband John Indian to the Reverend Parris of Boston in the Bay Colony." The words came with no difficulty. In fact, they seemed musical and strong. Gertrude stood as she said them. She thought about a sun-warmed island called Barbados. She thought of what it might have been like to have been sold for money and sent away to a cold and foreign place called Boston. It was all something like an Owl Game, only now she did not need to invent the story and the words. Instead she invented the feelings that went with them. Now that she knew the words by heart, the feelings began to come, too. When she finished, Nina sat up and clapped her hands.

"Oh Gertie, that was wonderful. You were wonderful."

Jessie sat staring at Gertrude. "You were fantastic! I never even realized what a great acting coach I am."

Gertrude smiled. She guessed Jessie was about to expand into a new career.

Jessie and Nina were eager to see the rest of the apartment, especially Albert's room.

"I don't believe it." Jessie counted the awards over Albert's desk. "I bet he buys them off some guy on Forty-Second Street."

Gertrude laughed. "Not Albert."

"Look at the books he reads." Nina was going through the shelf. "Everything is 'How to' and 'So You're Going to.' Doesn't he like stories?"

"Listen to me, Gertrude Hollings." Jessie put on her consultant face. "You have your hands full. This boy is an overachieving compulsive neurotic. He needs help. Open his mind and expose him to works of imagination."

"I'm trying my best."

"But you're still intimidated by him," Jessie guessed. "And you won't get anywhere that way. He has big problems."

"But Jessie," Nina squeaked, "since when is being perfect a big problem?"

Jessie scoffed, but Gertrude silently agreed with Nina.

By the time Eugenia returned home, Jessie and Nina were collecting their sweaters and jackets. "How nice to meet friends of Gertrude's," Eugenia said.

"Actually, I tutor her in remedial work and coach

her in drama." Jessie put out her hand. "Today I am happy to say we had an excellent session."

"Oh, well good." Eugenia looked baffled.

"I came to observe," Nina said hastily.

"I know you want to take Gertrude up to the country for the spring vacation, but she could make wonderful strides if she came to stay with us. In this work, continuity is the name of the game," Jessie said.

"It is?"

"She's doing so well, it would be a shame if she lost ground."

"But a vacation can be important, don't you think?"

"Not from tutoring."

"I see." Eugenia looked as if her face was about to go into a spasm.

"Bear it in mind." Jessie put up her hood.

"I loved your cookies." Nina waved.

"I'll bear that in mind, too," Eugenia said as she closed the door and burst out laughing. "What interesting friends you have, Gertie."

The next morning Nina whispered over Gertrude's notebook, "Have you heard? Jessie's officially going into the Drama Coach business. She's using me as a reference and telling people to check with me about the job she's done on you. She says when they see you in the play on Friday she won't be able to handle the mob."

"I don't know about that." Gertrude looked away.

Mrs. Delson walked up behind them. "A little less

conversation, girls. You're supposed to be doing those sheets."

"Oh, but I can't," Nina wailed. "The sentences are too hard."

Mrs. Delson leaned over to read her work. "They really aren't too hard for you, Nina. You just have to make an effort."

"I can't."

"Show me what you mean." Mrs. Delson pulled a chair in between Gertrude and Nina.

Gertrude put her head down on the table and closed her eyes. Olivia was trying on the wing protectors Oliver had made. "They're too heavy," she cried. "I can't fly with them, and especially not through burning hoops. Hoot hoooot hoooot."

Mrs. Delson turned sharply. "Gertrude, if you have nothing to do but hoot, why don't you go over your homework assignment?"

"I can't do it, it's too hard. I need help."

"I'm helping Nina now. Try it by yourself."

"I'll wait till my tutor helps me. I can't do it myself."

"How do you know if you won't try?"

"Because I know. I have this problem." She was exasperated. Mrs. Delson had forgotten her problem. Just because Nina had been wailing, *she* was getting the attention. "My words are all mixed up."

"I'm helping Nina now," Mrs. Delson repeated. "If you can't do your own work, don't make it impossible for Nina to do hers."

"Stop hooting," Nina grumbled.

Gertrude went to the library and read a picture book.

Mrs. Tausig said, "Aren't you interested in the ancient Greeks anymore?"

"It was too hard," Gertrude pouted.

Mrs. Tausig turned back to her file cards. After a while, Dr. Phelps came in to speak with her. They whispered for a moment and then they both looked at Gertrude. Dr. Phelps went over to her table.

"Come into my office for a minute, Gertie," she said cheerfully. "Let's have a chat."

Reluctantly Gertrude followed her. She didn't like being seen going to the school psychologist's office. She didn't want a "chat."

"Are you feeling a little lonely with your parents away?" Dr. Phelps said.

In fact, this thought had not occurred to Gertrude at all. Lonely? Gertrude stared at her. "No."

Dr. Phelps took an assortment of dolls out of a box on her desk. There was a man doll, a lady doll, and a small girl doll. "Would you like to play with these for a little while?" she said. "Make a game with them."

"I don't know how to do that," Gertrude said stupidly.

"I understand you're very imaginative," Dr. Phelps said. "Use your imagination and make up a game with the dolls." She held her pencil over a pad as if she would begin to write.

"I don't feel like playing now." Gertrude stood up. "I have some work to finish in my vocabulary sheets."

She hurried back to her classroom happy to have her work to get back to, with or without Mrs. Delson's help.

Later at lunch Jessie stormed up to her table. "I warned you to watch out about making noises and acting like a dope. You'll get a reputation that neither of us needs. Learning problems do not necessarily mean social problems. How will you ever make any progress with Albert if you allow yourself to carry on like this?"

"I am making progress," Gertrude replied defensively.

Jessie looked dubious. "Not if you hoot and act like a creep."

It was four-fifteen when Gertrude returned to Eugenia's. Albert was still working at his desk. The scratch-scratch of his pencil never stopped. In spite of what she had said to Jessie, she doubted she would ever succeed with him.

It was Friday. She had nearly used up her first week at the Nugents'. There were two weeks left in which to work. Gertrude sat down on her bed and thought of her mother and father till her eyes were wet. Dr. Phelps was right. She *was* lonely for them. Mrs. Delson must have told Dr. Phelps about her hooting. Maybe they all thought she was a screwball. She wriggled her feet under the covers and pulled the quilt over her head. She didn't want to get out of bed for a long time. Not till her parents were home, not till Jessie and Nina would go away, not till a weekend with the Nugents up at Hillside had passed. She closed her eyes. Albert's pencil stopped scratching. In a moment his horrible horn would begin. She braced herself for it. But instead she heard his footsteps. She raised herself on one elbow to see what he was doing. She had found that in the reflection from the glass over her cornflower pictures she could observe him through the open bathroom doors without his knowing it. She watched him enter the bathroom and look around. He marched up to the bathtub, an expression of dread on his face, yanked back the shower curtain, and leaped away as if he had seen a monster.

Why was he so frightened of the bathtub?

When the answer dawned on her, Gertrude nearly fell off her bed. Albert had believed her. He really was afraid that there was a thunderbolt in the tub. Even though he smirked and teased and called her Gertrude the Loser. This may not be rapport and respect, but it was Power.

Suddenly she couldn't wait for the weekend to begin.

❧ Twelve ❧

SATURDAY morning at Hillside, Albert was in a bad mood. The large kitchen window of the country house looked out over an expanse of lake, mountain, and sky. Gertrude and Albert sat facing this window while Eugenia squeezed oranges and Bruce read the local paper and ate prunes. There was a thick mist rising from the lake. The mountaintops looked as if they were floating above the clouds.

"I'm missing Josh Mallory's birthday at the Cattleman Restaurant," Albert said. "There were going to be clowns and a magician and balloons and a ride in a stagecoach."

"Can't kids amuse themselves anymore? Don't they know how to get together and have a good time without their parents paying a bunch of actors to show them how?" Bruce murmured.

"There's nothing to do up here," Albert persisted. "It's boring. It's a completely boring place."

"All of nature lies before you." Bruce waved one

hand at the window without looking up. "Its mystery and its beauty."

"Boring." Albert sipped the juice his mother had set before him.

"I have a little present for you which should make it less boring." Eugenia winked at Gertrude.

"A present? Is it just for me? Or to share?"

"You'll both need it, though I'm giving it to you to carry."

She searched in her handbag for a minute and withdrew a small unwrapped box and handed it to Albert. Inside the box was something that looked like a metal pocket watch. It was a compass.

Albert opened the lid of the compass and put it on the table. "What good is this?"

"It's perfect for exploring the woods and hills without fear of getting lost."

"Who wants to explore?"

"Really, Albert, you're being impossible." Eugenia picked up a section of the newspaper with disgust.

"Since you're not interested, may I use your compass?" Gertrude reached over her cereal bowl for it.

"Who said I wasn't interested?"

"Now you're interested because I am."

"My mother gave it to *me*." He grabbed it up and shoved it in his bathrobe pocket.

"You'll use it together or not at all," Bruce suddenly hollered. "Now get dressed, both of you, and get out of the house. Don't let me hear another word about clowns and balloons and being bored."

Albert and Gertrude got up from their chairs so fast they nearly knocked each other down. "I'll meet you with the compass in ten minutes," Albert said grudgingly on the stairs as they went up to their rooms to dress.

Gertrude's heart pounded. Everything was working out.

When they met ten minutes later, they were both in blue jeans, waterproof boots, and jackets. "Mine has a hood," Albert pointed out.

"Take mittens," Eugenia suggested. "These April days can turn very chilly."

"And something to eat," Bruce said in a conciliatory way, going into the kitchen to make sandwiches.

"I'm carrying the compass," Albert told Gertrude. "So you take the food."

"I've got to get a picture of this," Eugenia cried and ran off to get her camera.

Gertrude and Albert stood side-by-side on the planked deck steps scowling against the sunlight into Eugenia's camera. Gertrude could see the results now on the bulletin board: *Albie Goes for a Hike*.

"That is so cute." She pressed the lever. "Please be careful not to go too far and keep the house in view so you don't get lost."

"You gave us this stupid compass for that," Albert reminded her sourly.

They walked down the steps and up the short gravel driveway with Albert in the lead, straight toward the beginning of a thick wood that went nearly to the bank of the lake.

"Where are we going?" Gertrude asked.

"North." Albert consulted the compass and his watch. "For one hour we'll hike north. Then we'll turn around and hike south. That will get us home again."

"Are you sure?"

"It's right here," he said impatiently, pointing at the dial. "North. South." He strutted before her, letting the twigs and underbrush snap back from his legs so that they hit her thighs and chest with force. She was so eager to keep up with him that she could pay no attention to where they were going, or even how far they had gone. Aside from the underbrush, there were other problems. The ground was uneven and sloping. First it went steeply down and then up. There were stones that threatened to throw her off balance and patches of slippery snow. Even worse were the soggy areas where snow had melted and her foot sank into ice water up to the ankle. Thorny branches snagged at her trousers. She was sweating and breathing hard. Albert's back moved ahead of her like a relentless battery-operated toy. She thought he would never stop. Suddenly he turned around. His face was crimson and glistening with sweat. "Do you call this fun?" he demanded.

Gertrude shrugged.

"I could be at the Cattleman Restaurant with my friends."

"Well, you're not. You're here with me."

"Where's here? This dump?" He stamped, and water spurted over his boots. "Mud and mess and you. If it wasn't for you, I could have stayed in the city."

"That's not true."

"Yes it is. I heard my mother say she wouldn't let me sleep at Eddie Fringer's house and go to the birthday party because they'd be stuck having to entertain you alone. They dragged me up here so we could be together and I could learn what it's like to have a sister or a brother." His expression was one of pure contempt.

Gertrude sensed that this was her big moment. "Albert" — she put out a hand — "what could be more important in your whole life than learning how to get along with your brother or sister? Learning to share and to be flexible?"

He glared at her. "Share and be flexible with some screaming red wrinkled little creep? What are you talking about? Have you seen any babies?"

"They grow up." She avoided the question.

"Yes, they grow up to be like YOU. Eating my food, using my soap, reading my books, spying on my room."

Gertrude closed her eyes. This was bad. It certainly

wasn't respect. Maybe Albert hated her. She had a strong desire to shove his face into the wet leaves and sit on him till he said he was sorry. But no professional tutor would behave like that. She kept her eyes closed, hoping her urge to knock him down would pass quickly. She tipped her head back and opened her eyes so that she could see the sky through the bare high branches of the trees. The sudden movement of her head made her slightly dizzy. Sharp sunlight and the high patch of blue with a swift puff of cloud passing through it gave her the sensation of falling backward. Space between the branches seemed to be in flight. "Ennnnnn, ennn," Gertrude whined, taking advantage of the swaying sensation. She rocked on her boot heels, wondering what she should do next.

"Huh?" Albert said.

"Ennnnn, ennn."

"What?" He moved cautiously up to her and put a hand on her shoulder. "What's the matter with you?"

She made her eyes go glassy and strange and looked through him as if she were blind. Still rocking she raised her arms and filled her lungs with sharp cold air. In doing this she actually began to feel like an oracle. Strange and possessed, she could tell her face was changing. Albert was getting agitated. "Sun and trees and light and air enter me. Athena and Apollo and mighty Zeus, hear me. O Kition . . . speak through me . . .

"Albert, I'm Albert."

ahhhh."

"Albert?" She raised her brows and stared in icy remoteness. "What is it, Albert? What do you want?"

"I want you to know I'm Albert," he said with a rude little laugh. "You're Gertie and I'm Albert. Got it?"

"I'm Gertie, you're Albert?" she repeated in a sing-song. "Gertie, Albert . . . I am the Voice." She strung out *voice* and sang it in a high piercing cry. "You are Alllllbert," to the tops of the trees, like the cry of a hawk.

"Hey, cut that out." Albert reached his hand up as if to cover her mouth. "What's the matter with you, Gertie?"

"Through me, the gods and Kition speeeeak," she said, drawing out *speak* so that it was another shrill bird cry. From high above them a hawk screamed and wheeled beneath the clouds as if in answer. Albert stared up at the hawk. His face was pale.

This was better than an O.G. Much better. Gertrude could feel her power increase and take hold of him. Wait till Jessie heard this. She threw up her hands. "Speak through me, spirits of the gods." Then she lowered her voice to a hoarse whisper and swayed, closing her eyes as if she were listening. "O wretched, wretched one . . ."

"For your information, I am not O Wretched One. I'm Albert, you ding-a-ling." He sounded distressed.

"Wretched Albert."

"Me?"

"Albert." She raised her arms as she had when pretending to hold the thunderbolt. "Beware . . . beware."

"Beware of what?" He was perfectly still, leaning toward her at an angle.

"Beware of the Babe."

"The Babe? Are you nuts?"

"The Babe who will take . . ." She waited. ". . . your . . ." She waited again. ". . . place."

"Gertie," he shrieked, sounding so much like the hawk that it occurred to her that she might have gone too far.

She rubbed her eyes and pretended to come out of a trance. "What happened, Albert? Why are you looking at me like that?"

He was white as the clouds and there were blotches under his eyes. "What happened to you?" he breathed.

"I don't know. I felt sort of dizzy for a minute. Why, did I faint or something?"

"We have to go home, Gertie."

"Why? Is it an hour already?" She swung her arms casually. She felt so good, she could have walked all day.

"I don't know. I feel sick." He looked sick, too. In fact, he could hardly drag his feet and he kept stumbling. He gave her the compass to carry and let her walk first. Even at her slow pace he had trouble keeping up.

"Do you want to stop and eat our sandwiches?"

"I feel nauseous." He held his stomach and looked as if he might be sick. "Please, Gertrude, just get me home." His voice was a babyish version of itself. Gertrude could hardly believe the effect she had had upon him. They walked a bit more. Every time she turned back, he seemed to get weaker. She had to stop and wait for him to catch up.

"Is it much farther, Gertie?" He put out his hand and she took it.

"We'll be there soon." In fact, she wasn't sure of where they were going. She had not paid much attention when she had followed him in the first place. Just when she was beginning to worry, she saw the chimney of the house through a clearing of brush. She couldn't believe the power she had had over him. It made her feel light-headed with success. "Almost there, old boy," she called gaily.

As he tottered up the steps onto the deck, Eugenia came through the door. "Albert, what on earth happened to you?"

"I feel sick." He crumpled onto the top step.

"Darling." Eugenia knelt beside him with difficulty. Gertrude noticed for the first time how the jacket she wore stretched over her stomach. She took his pale face in her hands. "I think you may have a fever." She tugged Albert to his feet and, by supporting him under his arm, helped him into the house.

Gertrude watched them. Without warning, her feeling of success vanished. Suddenly she felt as sick as Albert looked. What sort of person was she? How could she have tricked him so? But who would have guessed that those oracle words would affect him? What if he told his parents? How would she explain it to them? She couldn't even explain it to herself. She met her aunt on the stairway. "Can I see Albert?"

"He's resting now. Perhaps after lunch. He may have a fever."

A fever? She had given Albert a fever?

After a lunch she could scarcely eat, Gertrude took a deck of cards into Albert's room. "Would you like to play a game of casino?" she asked gently.

His face turned toward her on the pillow, and he nodded. He watched with round sad eyes as she dealt the cards out on a tray table that straddled his knees. She recalled guiltily that only a few hours before she had wanted to shove his face into the dirt and sit on him.

"You know, Albert, having a little brother or sister could be a wonderful thing for you," she said softly.

"I don't want to talk about it."

He beat her three times at casino, but he didn't seem to care. "I'm tired," he said. "I need to take a nap."

Later in the day, a family named Robinson visited. Gertrude was relieved that Albert got dressed and came downstairs. Mrs. Robinson was a tall jolly woman who wrung Gertrude's hand and stood back to "feast my eyes on you." "I'm so happy to meet you, Gertie. I went to school right here in Hillside with your mother. When I look at you I can see her exactly. Dreamy Dora, we called her. She always had her shoes on the wrong feet and her dress on backwards. She spelled her name backwards, now that I think of it. She couldn't read time till the tenth grade. Do you remember, Eugenia, we had to tell her which way to turn in marching band, or she'd have ended up in the lake." She shook her head with wonder. "Whoever would have thought Dopy — I mean — Dreamy Dora would wind up writing a column in a national magazine?"

"Whoever would have thought she wouldn't?" Eugenia said defensively. "We all knew she was a late bloomer."

"And still waters run deep," Mrs. Robinson added in conclusion.

A late bloomer? Still waters run deep? Dreamy Dora? Dopy Dora? Gertrude was confused. Why hadn't they called her mother L.D., dyslexic? Why hadn't she been sent to a tutor? Hearing all these things made Gertrude limp with the desire to see her mother. She needed to talk to her. She needed to tell her what had happened to Albert and to herself. She needed to know more about Dreamy Dora. So much was happening. So much more could happen. How would she know what to do?

"Dinner is ready," Bruce said.

❧ Thirteen ❧

GERTRUDE was alarmed when Albert stayed in bed most of the next day. Late in the afternoon, Eugenia helped him dress and settled him gently in the back seat of the car beside Gertrude for the trip back to the city. In the city Bruce double-parked in front of their building so that Eugenia could assist Albert while Gertrude and her uncle carried in the bags.

"I'm calling Dr. Gardner," Eugenia said. "He's so weak."

They stood eyeing Albert, who leaned by the elevator door looking as if he were one of the lobby marble pillars. He didn't react to the comments about him except to close his eyes.

After dinner Dr. Gardner arrived. When he emerged from Albert's room with Eugenia and Bruce, he was shaking his head. "I can't find anything. Perhaps it will surface in a few days. In the meantime, I'll run these tests and see if they shed any light." He rubbed his chin.

"Has anything happened to him, some psychological shock or trauma? To tell you the truth, he seems depressed."

Eugenia frowned. "He went for a hike in the woods with his cousin Gertrude, and when they came back he could scarcely walk." She glanced up and saw Gertrude at the entrance to the hall. "Gertie dear, did anything happen to Albert in the woods? Something that scared him or upset him?"

Gertrude shook her head slowly.

"Did you two talk about something?"

She shook her head again. She couldn't look Eugenia in the eye.

The next morning Albert did not feel well enough to go to school. Eugenia was very concerned. "Still no fever and no symptoms, not even a rash. He's so sad and so weak," she said at breakfast.

"I have a new tutor today," Gertrude said, hoping to change the subject. "She called Mrs. Barnes and she lives on Eighty-Second Street."

"Oh yes, she phoned to confirm your appointment. Mrs. Barnes sounds very nice, Gertie."

"I hope she uses beans and gives treats."

"That would be nice, I'm sure," Eugenia said distractedly.

But when Gertrude arrived at Mrs. Barnes's apartment she saw no jar of beans anywhere.

"Hi, Gertrude." Mrs. Barnes was very crisp. "I've been eager to meet you. Please sit down and make yourself comfortable."

Gertrude sat down, but she was definitely not comfortable. Mrs. Barnes was tall and slender and gray-haired. She looked like the sort of person who wouldn't know what a Droste chocolate apple was. "You've made some wonderful progress lately. I've heard about your independent research in Greek mythology, and that your reading has really improved," Mrs. Barnes began. "I also learned that since you were taken out of the math workbooks and given sheets you haven't turned any of them in. Shall we have a look at the math homework?"

"I lost the math sheets."

"I see." She tapped a pencil on her desk and her cool gray eyes seemed to see past Gertrude to some spot where the truth about Gertrude lay hidden. "How about the vocabulary assignment? Do you have that with you?"

Gertrude poked in her pockets and took out the wrinkled, spotted word list. She handed it to Mrs. Barnes, who smoothed it on her desk. "Where are the beans?"

"I don't use beans for someone of your age." She looked up. "You are an intelligent and capable young woman, Gertrude."

"I'm dumb at school. I can't do a lot of the things."

"Yet I'm told you were able to handle the encyclopedia."

"That was special. I had to do it with somebody and it wasn't easy for me. I just did it because I really had to. I'm Learning Disabled, you know."

"Yes?"

"I have a problem with numbers." Gertrude was talking very fast. Why didn't Mrs. Barnes know all these things? "I see them backwards and upside down."

"You don't have to tell me. I have the same problem. We need to work a little harder, Gertie, but nobody ever died of that kind of work. In fact, we can even come out way ahead and that's fun." She winked. "So let's make a start on this assignment and you be sure to bring those math sheets next time you come."

Gertrude didn't like Mrs. Barnes. She was brusque and cold. She suddenly realized how much she liked Mrs. Crossman and felt a twinge of guilt for having taken for granted the jar of beans and the nice treats.

"I understand you have the leading role of Tituba in your class play. I'd like to hear you run through the part." She held the script. "Your teacher gave me a copy."

"I don't need that thing." Gertrude glared at the script. "I haven't used it for weeks. My teacher knows that." She was furious that Mrs. Barnes had done so much snooping about her. When she said her lines her anger made the words come out strong and clear.

"That was excellent," Mrs. Barnes interrupted. "You'll be a hit. I could listen to you all afternoon, but we're out of time." She put out her hand to take

Gertrude's. "I think we'll have fun working to-gether."

"Fun?" A few minutes later, Gertrude stood on the other side of Mrs. Barnes's closed door, staring at it, stunned. "Fun?" A boy got off the elevator and asked her to step aside. They watched each other while he rang the bell. Next case.

As she went out into the street, Gertrude's feelings of dismay began to give way to their opposite. The words clanged in her ears like celebration bells. "You are an intelligent and capable young woman, you know, Gertrude." She felt she could burst with the sounds of these words. She wanted to tell them to someone. Who? Her parents were in Greece. Eugenia and Bruce? Then she knew. She would tell Jessie.

When she arrived at Jessie's apartment, she found Jessie and her brother Alex watching TV. "We're just taking a break. I've been giving him his script." Jessie nodded at her little brother. "You should see the progress this kid has made. Let me show you." In the kitchen she pulled out a stack of notebooks and placed them on the table. "See how he's improved. Look at that *b*. He finally got it right. It was like pulling teeth."

"It was a lot worse," Alex hollered in. "It was horrible."

"My old tutor gave me treats," Gertrude said casually, "but my new tutor says I'm too smart and too mature for that. She says I am an intelligent and capable young woman."

"As long as you're satisfied," Jessie said coolly. "By the way, how are you doing with S.P.?"

"Can we speak privately?" Gertrude said. She had not realized how much she needed to tell Jessie what had happened over the weekend in Hillside. She hadn't realized that this was the real reason she had come.

When Gertrude finished the story, Jessie sat considering it for a while. Finally, she folded her hands like Dr. Phelps. "The only way to fix it is to teach him to make things up, so he understands how it is done."

"I don't follow."

"He won't believe you because he doesn't know how to do what you did. Give him a lesson in How to Pretend."

Gertrude recalled the afternoon Albert had heard her doing an O.G. and had pleaded with her to teach him — "How do you do it, Gertie?"

"Jessie, you're a genius," she said. "I'll tutor him in daydreaming."

"No charge," Jessie said.

When she returned to the Nugents' apartment, it was nearly five. This was one of Eugenia's teaching days. There was no sound of Albert's horn. Gertrude tiptoed down the hall and looked into his room. Albert lay on his side. His eyes were facing the wall. His hand was still on the cover.

"Are you sleeping?" Gertrude whispered.

"No." He watched her without moving his head.

"Listen, Albert, I was teasing you when I pretended I was the oracle and said 'Beware of the Babe.' "

"No, you weren't." He shook his head sadly.

"I can even teach you how to do it!"

"Is it like an O.G.?" He propped himself on his elbows.

"Yes, except we don't need the animals." She sat on the end of his bed. "Let's pretend that I am Olivia, the snowy owl. She has been caught by a wicked impresario named Boris Plink. He wants her to fly through three burning hoops for his show at Madison Square Garden. Olivia thinks she will burn her feathers. She's afraid."

"What do I do?"

"You can be Oliver, who is Olivia's friend in the next cage. You have made her protective wing shields out of feathers." Gertrude lunged forward and grabbed Albert's hands. "Oliver," she said in her high Olivia voice, "I can't do it. They are too heavy. Even if I make the first hoop, I'll fall into the second one. I know I don't have the strength."

Albert stared dumbly. A frown of concentration started on his brow. "Escape, Olivia," he hissed. "Escape."

"How could I? Hooot hooooot. These cages are so strong and the locks are iron."

"When they take you from the cage to do your act, fly upward . . . soar to the roof."

"What will I do then?"

"There is an opening . . ." He looked up at the ceiling. "Fly through it."

"Are you sure?"

"I will call upon all the owls in the woods. If they hear me they will lift the glass."

"How do we call them?"

Albert tilted his head back. "Hoooooot hooooooot," he cried.

The door opened and Eugenia peered in.

"I'm an owl," Albert yodeled. "Hoot hooooot hoot." He jumped out of bed and circled the room with his arms out stiffly at his sides like wings. "Hoot hoot."

"Does that make me an owl's mother?" Eugenia asked worriedly.

"We were acting," Gertrude explained.

"Yes, I know *you* are quite the actress, Gertie . . . you study it in your school. Albert, will you please get back into bed? This can't be good for you. You ought to be resting with a game of checkers or cards, not getting all worked up and pretending to be an owl."

Albert got back into bed. He looked embarrassed and sad.

"Maybe Albert could help me fix up my costume for Tituba," Gertrude suggested to cheer him up. "The play is on Friday."

"Now that does sound like fun." Eugenia was enthusiastic. "I'm sure we can find what you need in my closet."

"Mrs. Daniels said a simple long skirt and dark blouse would be best."

"I think I know just the thing. Come, Albert, let's costume Gertie for her play."

In her bedroom, Eugenia opened closets and drawers and rummaged for a moment before she drew out a long dark wool skirt. "It's down to my ankles so it should sweep the floor on you, Gertie."

Gertrude put the skirt on while Eugenia hunted for a brown jersey blouse. The combination of blouse and skirt made Gertrude appear older and taller. She was amazed by her reflection in the mirror.

"I'll wear dark makeup on my face," she said.

"Who would have thought it?" Eugenia marveled. "Albert, doesn't she look like a perfect Tituba?"

"That's because she *is* a witch," Albert said with certainty.

Eugenia laughed. "I hope that isn't what comes of play-acting and make-believe. The people of Salem believed in witches because they were ignorant and superstitious and hadn't the benefits of education and scientific knowledge."

"But Gertie *is* a witch." Albert was serious. "She can be an oracle, too. She can hear the voices of the gods when she's in the woods and predict the future."

"What?" Eugenia grew still with interest. "What happened in the woods?"

"She was the oracle. She swooned and she said I should beware of the babe."

Eugenia turned a stricken look on Gertrude. "You did that, Gertie?"

"I was joking," Gertrude murmured.

"A joke is supposed to be funny. This isn't funny at all."

"I thought he would know I was joking."

"Albert is very impressionable. He hasn't had nonsense and make-believe in his life. He doesn't understand it. He doesn't know the damage it can do."

Gertrude was suddenly filled with sympathy for her cousin. What was Eugenia saying? That there was something Albert was not supposed to be able to do? Did Albert have a label too? Make-Believe Disabled? Imagination Disabled? There were all kinds of labels to get stuck with in this world, Gertrude realized to her amazement. All kinds.

That night there was no Dinner Program. Gertrude and Albert ate spaghetti in the kitchen. Later, when they were back in their own rooms, Bruce and Eugenia dined alone with the door shut. There was no Homework Review. There were no Bed Preps. If she hadn't known she was in trouble, Gertrude would have enjoyed herself. She heard Eugenia and Bruce speaking in low voices with Albert in his room. She didn't try to eavesdrop. She didn't want to know what was going on.

In the middle of the night when the entire apartment was dark and even the lights in the courtyard had been extinguished, Gertrude was awakened by a sharp scream.

She jumped out of bed before she was even awake and ran to the sound. It was Albert, half asleep, his face contorted by dread, a thin moan still on his lips.

"Wake up," Gertrude shook him, "wake up, Albert!"

He opened his eyes, round and babylike and grabbed her arm. "They sent me away, Gertie. They sent me to Greece."

"No they didn't. It was a dream."

"They told me not to dream. They told me it was bad for me to daydream and believe in daydreams."

"You had a nightmare. Now forget it and go back to sleep."

"I can't." He seized her arm and held it tight.

Gertrude sighed. "Do you want to play a game of checkers? Maybe it will take your mind off your bad dream."

He lay back on his pillow and watched her set out the board and place the pieces. "If my parents knew we were doing this at two o'clock in the morning, they'd hoot," he whispered.

"Then we'd have to let them in on an Owl Game."

"But we wouldn't let them win."

"You don't win or lose in Owl Games."

They played three games of checkers. Albert won them all. He listed the scores on his card.

"Now it's time to go back to sleep." Gertrude yawned as she folded up the board.

"Maybe I'll have another bad dream."

"Forget it and go to sleep."

But when she returned to her own bed, she could not forget the look on Albert's face. What could she do? Jessie's suggestion hadn't worked. If a swooning act in the woods had gotten her into trouble, perhaps another swooning act in the woods would get her out of it. "Ennnn, lucky lucky Albert. You're going to get a Babe . . ." she mumbled into her pillow, and fell asleep.

❧ *Fourteen* ❧

WHEN Albert woke her up screaming for the third night in a row, Gertrude was nearly frantic. "Albert." She shook him awake, grateful that her aunt and uncle's bedroom was at the other end of the apartment.

"Oh, Gertrude." He grabbed her arms with both hands. "They left me on the train going far away and never told me."

"It was just another bad dream, Albert. It didn't happen."

"It's what the oracle predicted."

"I told you, I was pretending about the oracle. I was acting."

"And I told you, I don't believe you." He took her arm. "Remember, you said you put the thunderbolt in the bathtub?"

Gertrude nodded. "I was pretending then, too."

"That's what I thought, but that night when I took

my bath the pipes seemed to explode like they were angry and black water came out."

"It happens sometimes in these old buildings."

"No." He shook his head. "It was a warning. I got out of the tub. I won't use it anymore. You told me that the gods only speak through the priests when they're outside the house, out in the open. I looked it up and that was true, too."

As she opened the checkerboard for yet another middle-of-the-night game, Gertrude knew that her next "act" in the woods had better be good.

When Albert had won the game, he leaned back into his pillows and smiled wanly. "Isn't this fun, Gert?"

She had a curious desire to reach over and give him a comforting hug. Instead she arranged the covers about him. "Now go to sleep and try very hard not to dream." She thought of something else. "I'd also appreciate it if you would not tell your parents the stuff about the bathtub. I don't need more trouble." All that week, Bruce and Eugenia had treated her with polite coldness. One more misstep she felt would tip them into outright anger.

The next day in school, Nina appeared on the other side of her desk. She was so thin Gertrude was not aware of her presence until she was whispering in her ear. "You want to come to my house and look at my costume?" she said quickly, looking away as she spoke as if she could make a quick get-away in case she was rejected. "My mother put it together, and she thinks it's all right, but I don't know."

Gertrude was eager to see what Nina would wear. She had the part of Goody Good, the beggar woman who was accused of witchcraft along with Tituba and Goody Osborn.

"Meet me on the steps when school is out." Nina rushed away.

Later, waiting for Nina, Gertrude saw Jessie glaring at her from behind the outside door. She opened the door and bore down, sullenly. "I hear you're going home with Nina," Jessie said forbiddingly.

"Is that bad?"

"She'll tell you a lot of stuff about how I cut her hair and ruined her looks. I think you ought to hear my side."

"What's your side?"

"When she came to Bradwin, Nina was a mess. She wouldn't talk to anybody, sit with anybody, or do her work." Jessie narrowed her eyes. "Like you, only worse. She actually brought a stuffed panda to school in her knapsack."

Gertrude silently thanked heaven she had never taken Olivia as she had wanted to do.

"I thought she needed a new image, so I cut her hair. I really helped her. Once she had a new image, people noticed her. They felt sorry for her. They thought she looked awful. She made friends. She was one of my first real successes, but she'll never admit it. And now she invites you over and doesn't ask me."

Nina floated between them. "Do you want to come over, Jessie?" she whispered.

"I have an appointment." Jessie got very pink. "But thanks for asking."

Nina lived in an old, immense apartment with long hallways and many dark rooms. There were large paintings on the walls and even a few rugs that were hung from the moldings. "We live with my grand-mother," Nina said as if this would explain the rugs and the paintings and the general gloom. "My Granny gave me my animals. Some of them were hers and some of them were my mother's." The animals she spoke of were lovingly arranged on Nina's bed. They were beautiful stuffed creatures made in Germany where her grandmother had bought them. They had glass eyes and soft furry bodies. Most of them were bears and squirrels, but there were two pandas. "This is Toby." Nina held up one of the pandas. "And this is Tinker." She gave Gertrude the other. "They were my mother's, so they aren't too old. I don't have to be as careful with them as the others."

Gertrude couldn't believe it, Nina didn't know enough not to confess to playing with stuffed toys. "I make them into a village," Nina said. "It's called

Donora. It's on the side of a lake. I use my mirror for the lake." She began to set up the village on her bed.

"I have owls. I could bring them over sometime."

"Not when Jessie comes." Nina smiled. "She'd say we were babies and try to help us over it."

Nina took out the raggedy dress she would wear in the play.

"It's perfect," Gertrude said. "My aunt is helping me with mine." The thought of Eugenia made her sad. She wondered if she could tell Nina about her problems with the Nugents, but decided Nina wouldn't understand the way Jessie did. She would get nervous and pull on her hair. Everybody was different. She was glad she knew them both.

They sat on the bed and played with the animals until it was time to go home.

Friday morning Gertrude took Eugenia's long dark skirt and the brown jersey blouse to school with her in a shopping bag. She knew her lines so perfectly even Jessie was pleased. However, she could feel her heart beat and she carried the script rolled up in one hand like a good-luck piece.

Mrs. Daniels put a dark pancake makeup on her face and pulled her hair back under a thick brown scarf. "You look fine," she said. "Don't worry." But Gertrude could see the uneasy question lines on her brow. Mrs. Daniels had never heard her go through her lines with feeling and without the script.

"I hope you know when you come in," Chris Kinnel said testily. "Because if you don't, you throw me off."

"Don't worry about Gertrude; I'll prompt her if she needs me to," Mrs. Daniels assured him quickly.

They were all expecting her to have problems. She closed her eyes, crossed her fingers, and prayed she would surprise them.

The middle school classes filed into the room in two lines and sat down around the sides of the polished floor.

"I like your costume," Gertrude told Chris. He had a pilgrim hat made of cardboard and painted black. His white collar was construction paper. Nina looked just like a wretched beggar woman in her rags, and Goodwife Osborn had a white paper collar and wrinkles drawn all over her face. It seemed to Gertrude that in some way they had all been transported to Salem Village in colonial times. Mrs. Daniels had made little Billy Alton look just like a harsh and mean-spirited Reverend Parris. Clayton Fisk, who was very tall and dark, wore a white workshirt and trousers rolled above the knee. He looked like Tituba's husband, John Indian.

Mrs. Daniels made a short speech about the subject of the play and then Chris Kinnel stepped to the front of the stage with his hands stiffly at his sides he began to recite his part. Gertrude did not need prompting. She was no longer Gertrude Hollings, but Tituba the slave. She took two steps forward and gazed out over the heads of the audience seated on the floor. "I am Tituba," she began, "from the sun-warmed island of Barbados where my mistress sold me with my husband John Indian to the Reverend Parris of Boston in the Bay Colony." She was as lost in her role of Tituba as she would be as Olivia in an O.G. The words came to her from her mind, not from a printed sheet of paper. They were her words and she gave them her own feelings. She could see that the faces of her audience were attentive and still. They gasped when she was accused of witchcraft. They laughed when she said something that was supposed to be funny. She felt a power over them. The sense of this power filled her like a wonderful bubble. They were a room full of Alberts. When the play was over, the middle school stood up to applaud.

"Gertrude, Gertrude." Mrs. Daniels rushed up on-stage. "You were fantastic."

For the rest of the day, teachers and classmates came up to her to tell her how good she had been as Tituba.

"Don't forget to tell them who coached you," Jessie glared.

"Oh, yes," Gertrude said loudly whenever she could, "Jessie Bogues was my coach."

Nina pulled on her hair. "I may be interested in drama coaching, Jess, but I have to check with my mother."

Jessie nudged Gertrude. "Tell her how awful you were when we started and how I even squeezed in some remedial math."

"I do not need remedial math," Nina said. "What I'm afraid of is more remedial haircutting."

"I wouldn't work with you unless I did an evaluation first," Jessie said hotly. "I may be too busy."

"An eval-u-a-tion." Nina rolled her eyes. "You never did an evaluation on my hair."

When she got home from school, Gertrude found a letter from her parents. They were the ones who had gone away, yet she felt she was the one who had traveled and changed. She was not the Gertrude who had said goodbye to them only two weeks before. She had a new tutor and a new friend. She had been a success in acting class and a failure at Albert's house. Two weeks could have been a year.

And so, darling Gerts, we hope you aren't still angry with us for leaving you behind, but we're sure you realize how busy this trip has been. Daddy found pieces of your math homework inside the collar of his shirt this morning. We had to laugh. It was like a message from our girl. Have you washed any assignments lately? We can't wait to see you, sweety. We miss you. . . . Love and Kisses.

Gertrude folded the letter and looked out the window at the pale chilly April afternoon. Albert had nightmares about his parents leaving him — she had no bad dreams and her parents *had* left. She was proud of this. She could hear Eugenia and Bruce in the kitchen deciding what foods they would pack for their week at Hillside. She could hear Albert in his room packing up some books and papers. She was gathering her thoughts and reviewing her plans. She had to do as good a job on her cousin in the woods as she had done as Tituba on the school's basement stage. Did one success follow another? She hoped so. A great deal depended upon it.

❧ *Fifteen* ❧

SATURDAY morning at breakfast Gertrude looked out the window. The sky was clear. No mist hung over the lake as it had the week before. Eugenia was at the counter squeezing oranges. Bruce was reading the local paper and sipping coffee. Albert was gazing into space. "Where's my compass?" he suddenly asked.

"I think you left it on your dresser," Eugenia said uneasily. "Why?"

"I want to take another walk with Gertie."

"You do? Are you sure? The McGoons are coming for lunch with their three girls."

"We'll be back in plenty of time if we get started now." Albert checked his thick wristwatch. "Three hours at least." He went to get the compass.

"Gertrude," Eugenia said as soon as he was gone, "no monkey business — promise me."

This time Bruce did not offer to make sandwiches and Eugenia did not take pictures of them. Instead, they both stared worriedly out the kitchen window as Gertrude and Albert made their way into the woods.

"We'll do what we did last time," Albert said without turning to look at her. "One hour north and one hour south." After a moment he added, "I want you to know, Gertie, I'm not scared about what the oracle will say."

She scrambled along behind him, hoping she would recognize the spot where the idea of the oracle had hit her the week before. "Could you slow down, Al?" she panted. "And please hold the branches for a minute so I'm not always getting whacked in the face."

To her surprise, he did as she asked. She remembered that the spot she was looking for had been on a small rise after a steep descent. There had been an opening in the underbrush and a heap of leaves, as if some animal had gathered them for a purpose. She recollected a cross-hatching of thorny twigs that had ripped at the cuffs of her jeans when she rocked back and forth. These were the sorts of "signposts" her parents always joked her about "reading," when she got actual street signs and numbers all mixed up. A heap of leaves, thorny twigs, and a small rise of earth were clear in her mind. Before long she knew they had arrived. Something like stage fright made her heart pound.

"Albert." She stood still while he kept walking with his head down. "Albert." She lowered her voice and drew out his name so that he turned immediately.

"Gertie? Is it happening?"

"Ahhhhh, Alberrrt," she crooned and lifted her brows in what she hoped was an expression of great joy. "Ahhhh, Alberrrt, listen to me."

"I am, I am." He came in closer to watch her.

She closed her eyes tight and swayed. Then she opened them wide, and, moving her head from side to side in rhythm to a strain of music that only she could hear, she smiled. "Oh, Alberrrt."

"Yes?"

She gazed at him evenly, and saw to her dismay that he was searching her face as if it were a math problem he had to solve. She began to sway more recklessly. "Good news, Albert. Goooooooood news."

"What's the good news?"

"Love and Joy and Friendship."

"Love and joy and friendship?" His frown deepened.

"Love and Joy and Friendship are all in your golden future." She nearly lost her balance and fell down. "Kition has spoken!"

He reached out a hand to steady her. "You can stop flopping around now."

"What happened? What? Was I dizzy again?"

"You told me that I would have love and joy and friendship and all that baloney."

"I did?"

"And you were hamming it up so I would stop having bad dreams and waking you in the middle of the night and getting you in trouble with my parents."

She felt as if the entire woods had stood up and yelled, "Booooo." She had failed by going too far. By being obvious. She had been a bad actor. "Why didn't you believe me this time?"

"I don't know." He shrugged and looked at the ground. "I can tell when something is true. It isn't your fault. You were trying. I could see that. It just wasn't true."

They walked along in silence for a while. "Why wasn't it true this time?"

"If *you* were getting a brother or sister, what do you think you'd believe? All those books they give me about *Your Trip to the Doctor, Your Trip to the Zoo, So You're Going to the Hospital* — they're never right. When the real thing happens you see that the books were wrong. I'm always getting prepared for things that turn out to be different." He stopped walking and turned to face her. "Like you."

"Me?"

"They told me how great it would be when you'd come to stay at our house. They told me I would have someone to play casino with and Monopoly. They told me it would be like having a friend around all the time."

She hung her head. No wonder he was so put out with her. "We play checkers."

"You always lose. You don't even care. I would never have picked you for a friend, Gert."

The sun went behind a cloud, the sky darkened, and the air turned as chilly as her spirits. "I wouldn't have picked you either."

"They can't guarantee me anything about the baby they'll get. They don't know who's coming."

"That's true." Gertrude had to agree. "You don't get people to order. That's why you have to learn to bend a little." She bent a little as if to show him. "Maybe I don't play cards with you. But there were other things..."

"What?"

"We take these walks in the woods," she said hopefully. "We played checkers at two o'clock in the morning."

"Yeah." He looked even more dejected. "It's time to walk home."

"Can I do the compass?" Gertrude was surprised when he handed it to her without a word. Holding the warm metal disk was comforting. She squinted her eyes as if figuring out something very complex. In fact, the points and the black lines and letters confused her. She took the lead, which made her feel important. Albert followed. As they walked she held the compass in front of her. In her mind she began an Owl Game. Olivia and Oliver had escaped Boris Plink and were in the woods looking for owl friends.

"Did you say something?" Albert asked.

"Not really."

"This doesn't seem to be where we were before." Albert stopped and turned in a complete circle.

"It says south." She wrenched herself out of being Olivia and handed him the compass.

"No, it doesn't," Albert burst. "You've been walking us east. We're lost."

"I just got confused." Gertrude thought she would faint. She hadn't been paying attention.

Albert was furious. "I never should have let you take the compass. You weren't paying attention. Your mouth was moving. You were daydreaming."

"Can we sit down a minute, please?" She sat because her knees were too weak to hold her up. Once she had been lost coming home from school. All the buildings had looked alike. She couldn't tell one corner from another. She mistook right for left. Now all the trees looked alike. The ground offered no clues. Her chest filled with panic.

Albert squatted beside her and studied the compass. "Let's start to walk south and see what happens." He had to pull her to her feet. It wasn't a hike, but more of a stagger and stumble. After a while, Albert stopped. "It's so overgrown. I don't know where we are." He held the compass up and stared at it the way he'd stared at her when she was an oracle.

Even though she was confused, Gertrude knew one thing for certain. "The compass isn't going to help us," she said. "So stop looking at it."

He turned his head from side to side and gaped at the trees and squinted up at the sky. His white face had become transparent. Little blue veins showed under the skin of his brow. "What do we do then, Gertie?"

"Let's sit down and think about what we did." She managed to say this just as her knees gave out again.

"What did we do?"

"Clues, we need clues." Clues were what helped her when she got lost in the jumble of letters that went the wrong way and numbers that swam upside down. The clues her tutors had helped her find over the years and the ones she had figured out for herself had guided her out of panic when a nine looked like a six or she read the word *map* as *pam*. The birthmark on her right wrist, the vaccination mark on her left arm. The feel of her sandpaper letters, their roughness, was something she could sense with her fingertips if she closed her eyes. Clues could help you out of confusion. She closed her eyes. "We went up for a while and then we went down a little bit and then we went for a long time." She opened her eyes and looked at where they were. "We're still walking uphill. Let's start to go down."

"But that's north."

"We don't know how many times we turned." They began to walk down. After a while, Gertrude noticed an outcropping of stones. They weren't random stones. They looked as if they had been stacked by hand. "That must be an old wall," she said. "Let's follow it. It may lead us to another wall."

Albert checked his watch. "It's one o'clock. The McGoons are there. They all must be eating lunch."

"No, they aren't," Gertrude realized. "They're too worried about us."

"Maybe they made a search party."

"Not yet." She found an apple in her jacket pocket and offered it to Albert. He took a bite, but couldn't swallow.

"I can't eat, Gertie."

"Try. We may be hiking for a long time."

"What happens if we never get out of here? These woods go on for miles and miles. We could be lost till it turns dark. It will get cold. There are bears."

She stood up. "That stone fence will lead to another fence. If we follow it downhill we'll get out of the woods." Gertrude took the lead, and Albert followed. They tried to keep to the stone fence, but at times the underbrush prevented them from following it closely. Albert looked at his compass and said they were off course. Gertrude said they had done so much turning and twisting that there was no "course."

"It's nearly two o'clock," Albert said when they paused to rest for a moment. "Do you think they've sent out a search party yet?"

"I think that the stone wall divides at that tree," Gertrude pointed excitedly. One section of the fence continued old and crumbled, but the other was new and mended. "We'll follow the new fence."

"I thought learning disabled meant you have no sense of direction."

"If you don't have direction sense, you need common sense," Gertrude said, knowing it for the first time.

They followed the new fence until it turned onto a dirt lane which led to a blacktop road.

"This is Tucker Road," Albert gasped. "There's the sign for Younger's Apples. We're found, Gertie." He ran toward her and without warning wrapped both his skinny arms around her.

She picked him up with a whoop, and then he picked her up. "Hooray," he said.

"Hip hip hooray," they shouted and spun each other around.

"We're found." Gertrude planted a kiss on Albert's soft cheek.

❧ Sixteen ❧

GERTRUDE was not prepared for the scene that greeted them as they approached the house. In fact, it struck her as funny and made her smile. There was Eugenia standing on top of the picnic table on the deck with a pair of binoculars to her eyes. Bruce was holding what looked like a homemade bullhorn to his lips calling out their names. "Albert . . . Gertrude." There was a cold, unhappy-looking couple in Irish sweaters and plaid pants squinting into the woods and three girls arranged like steps on the picnic bench eating from a bag of potato chips.

When Eugenia sighted Gertrude and Albert stumbling up the driveway, she dropped her binoculars, jumped off the table, and ran toward them. "Where have you been? We called the Troopers. You've given us the scare of our lives."

Bruce strode up behind her. "Eugenia." He put a hand on her shoulder to stop her, but she was too upset.

"What have you done? Where did you go? I told

you to be back at noon. That was two and one half hours ago."

"We went to see the oracle again," Albert began.

"THE ORACLE?" Eugenia yelped. Then she turned to Gertrude. Her face was flushed with feeling. "You've done it again, Gertrude. That mumbo jumbo you torment Albert with. I told you how we felt about that. I told you that it is dangerous and mischievous. You have gone too far." Her eyes blazed and her voice began to waver and rise. She was too overworked to continue speaking, and so turned on her heels and ran toward the house.

"Why don't you two wash up for lunch and say hello to our guests?" Bruce said. "They've been waiting for you and it would be nice if you'd apologize. They're probably starving."

Eugenia did not look at Gertrude once all through the stiff and painful lunch. Even though the sun poured through the large window and flooded the cheerful plant-filled room with light, Gertrude felt darkness all about her.

Across the table from her were the three McGoon girls. They stared blankly or whispered and giggled among themselves. Gertrude exchanged a look with Albert. It said, "We're in trouble here."

"Please pass the lemonade," Albert said.

"It's all gone." Gertrude picked up the jug. "I'll get you some more."

"No, that's okay. I'll get it, Gertie."

They both got up to refill the pitcher. In the kitchen Gertrude broke out ice, while Albert mixed a frozen cylinder of juice with water. "What do you think will happen?" Gertrude said.

"Mom is very upset. On a scale of one to ten, she is upset to twelve."

Gertrude recalled her own mother's anger. It was usually in the form of a blow-up, something like a firecracker. Aunt Eugenia, however, appeared to be burning slowly, like a red-hot coal.

"But don't worry," Albert said worriedly.

The lemonade was ready. Reluctantly they returned to the dining room. Gertrude saw her aunt's troubled gaze follow them as they took their seats. She felt as if she were alone with Albert on a raft in a turbulent sea.

After lunch the McGoons went for a walk with Bruce around the lake.

Eugenia said, "Albert and Gertrude will stay here to help me clean up the lunch dishes. I don't want them leaving the house."

Gertrude and Albert cleared the table while Eugenia put food away and loaded the dishwasher. "Sponge off the countertops," she told Gertrude, "and get the crumbs off the table. I have phone calls to make. When you're done, there are some things we will discuss."

With a feeling of foreboding Gertrude sponged the table twice and then helped Albert clean the counters.

She polished the toaster and all the little knobs on the stove. "What's going to happen, Albert?"

"I think it's a punishment," he said grimly.

"What kind of punishments do you get?"

"In the city, I'm grounded, or I can't watch TV. But there is no TV up here, and I can't go anyplace anyway. How could I be grounded?"

"Grounded up here could mean being planted in the ground like a bush," Gertrude suggested, hoping to make Albert laugh.

He didn't.

"Or maybe, since there's no TV, they could forbid you to watch the view."

He did laugh at that. "No view for you today, young man," he imitated Eugenia. "We're pulling the shades down."

"Aw, pulease, Mom," Gertrude began to clown, "can't I even watch the sunset? I have to watch the sunset or I won't be able to follow tomorrow's show."

"Absolutely not." Albert wagged his finger. "Especially not the sunset. The sunset is not suitable for a child your age." At this they nearly doubled over laughing. But Eugenia walked in and suddenly they remembered how rotten they felt.

"Excuse me," Eugenia said. "I'm sorry to interrupt your hilarity, but I must speak with you, Gertrude." She paused and took a deep breath which seemed to cause her pain. "I don't understand what happened here today, or, for that matter, the last several days. My household, which has always run in a smooth and orderly manner, has been turned upside down. I never dreamed such problems would arise when I told your parents that I would look after you, Gertrude. I cannot sacrifice Albert's health and happiness to your visit. I have spoken to Mrs. Bogues, your friend Jessie's mother. She says that you can stay with them for the next week until your parents return. The McGoons will drive you back to the city this afternoon."

Gertrude and Albert did not look at one another. Out of the living-room window, Gertrude saw the McGoons and Bruce standing on the deck admiring the view.

"I don't want Gertie to leave," Albert said. "We're friends. I like Gertie being here. We did everything together. It's not her fault everything was upside down." He thought a moment. "And I like it upside down."

"What you like may not be what's best for you, Albert."

Bruce came through the sliding glass door and stood against the bookshelf.

Eugenia turned towards him. "I have just told Gertrude that I have made arrangements for her to return to the city with the McGoons this afternoon. She can stay with her friend Jessie Bogues. I told Gertie that we are not blaming her, but her visit here has not worked out."

"Yes it has," Albert objected.

"Did you hear your mother?" Bruce said.

Eugenia pursed her lips and looked at the floor. "Go upstairs, Gertrude, and get your things together."

It was not difficult to pack. She had scarcely unpacked. She remembered the little pomander balls tied with ribbon and Eugenia's words of welcome only two weeks before. What had happened?

Albert knocked on the door. "I don't want you to go, Gertie," he said. "It's my fault that they're sending you away. If you get sent away, I should be, too. I tried to tell them, but they won't listen to me. I want you to stay."

She continued to fold her things into the suitcase. "They think that I'm bad for you. They think that I prepared you in reverse for the baby, and that I did it on purpose. I gave you nightmares and worked you up. I didn't know that you'd believe everything I told you and take it so seriously. I had no idea you'd be so . . . so gullible."

"I'm not gullible," Albert protested.

Gertrude looked up from her packing. "Then would you please tell that to your parents? It might help. I can't think of anything that would."

"Kition," Albert said slowly. "Kition could help."

"What? Who? What are you talking about?"

"Kition. Fourth century B.C. You know, the one who gave you the power."

"Oh, Albert," Gertrude wailed. "You do believe every dumb thing I make up. You're hopeless."

He turned on his heels and left the room.

But all the way to the city, wedged between Mr. and Mrs. McGoon in the front seat of their car, it was Gertrude who felt hopeless. She wished she had Albert's faith in the nonsense she'd invented for him. She couldn't even distract herself with an O.G. As they approached the city, she thought of going to stay with Jessie. Jessie would want to know what had happened. She could just imagine how eager Jessie would be for the "whole story." Gertrude vowed not to tell her a single thing. This was a story she would only tell her parents. Suddenly she missed her mother and father so much she could hardly bear it. She needed to go home, to run to her mother's room and tell her about Eugenia and Albert and all the things that had happened. The McGoons' car pulled off the highway. She could see the water tower of her building. She rubbed the key that hung on a string around her neck and that she had never taken off. She was not going home, but to Jessie Bogues and a million questions. What had Eugenia told them about her? Something awful she was sure. She pinched her lips together. She would tell them nothing.

The minute Gertrude set foot in the Bogueses' front hall, Jessie grabbed her arm. "The whole story, Hollings, from beginning to end with nothing left out."

"Gertie's had a long day," Mrs. Bogues said. "Leave her alone." Then she turned a kindly smile on Gertrude. "Don't pay any attention to Jessie. We certainly aren't expecting you to give us a report on your troubles."

The apartment was filled with the smells of browning onions and mushrooms and cooking tomatoes. Mrs. Bogues was making manicotti. Mr. Bogues had given her a pasta machine for her birthday. Alex was watching television, and Vicki, Jessie's half sister, was doing her fingernails on the floor. Gertrude was suddenly seized with the desire to tell everyone in the room what had happened to her at Hillside.

"I can't eat any pasta," Vicki said. "I'm on a diet and I've got to squeeze into my new jeans tonight. I'm going out with Cliff."

"I'll tell you about what happened at Hillside," Gertrude said.

"Not now." Jessie stood up. "We have to watch Vicki get ready."

Vicki blew on her nails and screwed the cap onto the bottle of polish. "Okay, let's go." She got up, gracefully flicking her long hair to the side of her neck.

"Come on, Gert. You have to see this." Jessie beckoned Gertrude to follow her into the bedroom.

Gertrude was disappointed. Did Jessie want to hear about Hillside, or had she completely forgotten? They sat on the twin beds watching Vicki put color rub and glitter drops around her eyes. She stuck little feathers into her hair. A piece of her hair was dyed light pink.

"She looks like a fruitcake." Alex poked his head through the door.

"No, she looks like a clown," Jessie said.

"Aren't they mean, Gertie?" Vicki laughed. "You would never say anything like that. You're too nice."

"Nice? My aunt and uncle sent me away. They don't think I'm nice. They think I'm awful."

"Your aunt told my mother you were a bad influence on Albert," Jessie said. "She didn't say you were awful."

"I think Gertie is nice," Vicki repeated. She was glossing her lips.

"I told him these fantastic stories and he believed me. I never really thought he'd believe me."

"That's because you're a good actress," Vicki said. "People believe you. It's a kind of power."

"A power?" Gertrude marveled. It sounded like Zeus and his thunderbolt.

"Do you have a need to tell us about your traumatic experience in the country?" Jessie asked Gertrude.

"I'll bet she'd rather let me make her up," Vicki said.

"Me first." Jessie pushed her face forward.

What was this? Gertrude was amazed. Didn't anyone want to hear the true story of what had happened to her at Hillside?

❧ *Seventeen* ❧

I
N the morning Gertrude and Jessie lay in their beds
listening to Mr. and Mrs. Bogues getting ready for
the day. There was the whistle of the kettle and the ping
of the toaster oven and the smell of bacon and eggs
frying.

"No school on Monday." Jessie stretched and giggled.
"A whole week of no school at all." She rolled onto her
stomach and sighed. "I just can't get over it, Gertie. You
really did it."

"Did what?"

"Zapped horrible Albert."

"He's not horrible." Gertrude curled up as the first
wave of misery rolled over her. "And I didn't want to
zap him. I just wanted to establish rapport and respect,
like you said."

"Respect and rapport are one thing. But I never told
you to scare the daylights out of him. I got *you* into
tutoring without doing that."

"I was supposed to help Albert love the idea of his sibling. Instead I gave him nightmares and made him sick."

"That's ridiculous. You can't do that to a person. A person does that to himself."

"Remember that Vicki told me last night about having power?" Gertrude turned her face to the wall.

"I think you take yourself too seriously." Jessie got out of bed. "Let's eat."

In the kitchen, Mr. and Mrs. Bogues, Vicki, and Alex were at the table. Mr. Bogues was eating pancakes, eggs, and bacon, Mrs. Bogues a dish of bran, and Vicki was drinking a glass of Diet Alba. Alex was finishing the leftover manicotti.

"There's plenty of pancake batter," Mrs. Bogues said cheerfully. "How do you feel this morning, Gertrude?"

"So far so good," Jessie answered for her. "Vicki says Gertrude's got special powers."

Gertrude shot her a look over the bowl of batter.

"What does that mean?" Mrs. Bogues asked.

"It means she got kicked out of her aunt's house," Jessie said, ignoring Gertrude's pinched mouth and narrowed eyes.

"Now Jessie, don't put it that way," Vicki objected. "I said that being a good actress was having a kind of power."

"And Gertrude didn't get kicked out as far as I know," Mrs. Bogues put in. "Her aunt told me it hadn't worked out between Gertrude and her cousin."

"I started it, though," Gertrude said.

"I'm sure it took two."

"Her cousin Albert is an anal compulsive neurotic," Jessie explained.

"He is not."

Vicki held up the fashion section of the *Times*. "An Indian conch belt. If I had one, I could make my last year's denim smock look like this year's tunic." She pointed to a picture of a model in a loosely belted denim tunic.

"Fifty bucks?" Mr. Bogues exclaimed. "How about using last year's belt?"

"Because it looks like last year. I want to look like this year."

"I wish *I* could look like last year," Mrs. Bogues sighed.

Vicki turned back to her magazine in disgust.

"If she went to a school where they wore uniforms she'd avoid this clothes hang-up," her father said.

"They belt uniforms too, Daddy."

"They belt spoiled kids," Mr. Bogues punned, so that Vicki groaned and Alex bent over laughing.

The telephone rang. "I think it's for me." Vicki leaped from her chair, but Mrs. Bogues reached for the phone from where she sat. She said "hello" and then an expression of deep concern furrowed her brow. "Oh no," she gasped and glanced at Gertrude. "Do you want to speak to her?" She handed the receiver across the table. "It's your aunt Eugenia."

The pancake in her mouth suddenly tasted like felt, but she swallowed it and took the phone.

"Gertrude," Eugenia's voice crackled with worry. "When Albert didn't come down to breakfast this morning, we looked in his room and found he was gone. Can you tell us where he might be?"

"He never said anything to me."

"Do you think he would have gone back to the woods for more of that hocus-pocus?"

"Did he take his compass?"

"No, but he took his entire cash register bank. It's heavy."

"He wouldn't need money if he went into the woods."

"If you hear from him, Gertrude, please let me know right away. I'll call you later." Eugenia hung up.

"Have you any idea where he is, Gertie?" Mr. Bogues asked.

Gertrude shook her head. "I wish I did."

"Some special powers," Jessie scoffed.

After breakfast the sky darkened. Rain spattered the windows of Jessie's bedroom. Vicki's friend Diane arrived, and they set out to look for Japanese umbrellas. Mr. and Mrs. Bogues went to visit a relative in the hospital, and Alex went to the Danny-O Sports Club.

"Are you girls going out today?" Mrs. Bogues called from the door. "There are some good movies in the neighborhood."

"We could have a tutoring session," Jessie suggested. "Unless you'd rather play Monopoly."

What a choice! "Monopoly." Gertrude shrugged, immediately sure that she had made a mistake.

Jessie took the game very seriously. "Pay attention," she snapped. "You're not keeping your money so you can count it. Look, it's just flopping all over the place. You aren't concentrating."

"I don't like to play games that I always lose."

Jessie looked grim and put down the dice. "You win. I can't play with somebody who wrinkles up the bills. Let's go to the movies."

The phone rang, but when Jessie answered it, the other party hung up. Gertrude didn't say anything. She knew it was Albert.

At the movies they met Chris Kinnel and Lewis Alter. "I already saw this show twice," Lewis said, pointing to a poster for *Superman II*. "If I see it again, I'll be able to fly."

"No, you'll just end up wearing glasses like Clark Kent," Jessie said.

"Maybe Mrs. Daniels will let us do a Superman improvisation," Chris said to Gertrude. "You could be Lois Lane."

She was so pleased she nearly forgot all about Albert being out in the rain.

When they returned from two hours of *Superman II*, Mr. and Mrs. Bogues were in the livingroom sipping drinks and listening to the radio. "Your aunt called again," Mrs. Bogues said. "The police say that someone spotted Albert at the train station this morning. He was buying a ticket to New York. Your aunt and uncle are on their way back to the city."

Gertrude pulled on the boot she had been taking off. She zipped up her jacket and opened the front door.

"Where are you going?" Jessie said.

"I have to find him."

"You know where he is?"

Gertrude didn't answer. She was out the door and running to catch the self-service elevator before it closed.

"Wait," Jessie called just as the door banged shut on her face.

Gertrude didn't wait. It was late. She hadn't a minute to lose.

❧ Eighteen ❧

A CLUSTER of people were collecting their coats and umbrellas to one side of the museum entrance. Gertrude pushed through the crowds that were milling about the information desk and nearly ran past the museum shop, a planting of orchids, and the ticketseller turnstiles.

"What's your rush?" a guard said as she raced through the gallery of marble busts of Roman copies and frescoes from the walls of ancient houses. Even before she entered the long, high, arched gallery, she saw a small, loosely knit group of adults and children gathered around the sarcophagus of Kition. What they were observing, however, was not the sarcophagus, but Albert Nugent. Albert stood beside the sarcophagus with his hands clasped on his thin chest and his head bowed. He looked as if he were praying.

"Do you think it's some new sect?" a woman asked her companion.

"They get them awfully young."

"Albert," Gertrude said. "What do you think you're doing?"

He looked up and blinked. "Asking for help." He smiled. "And it worked."

"It didn't work. I happened to figure out where you'd be."

"It answered my questions." He patted the stone affectionately. "Kition heard."

"You know, I think you're turning into some sort of religious nut." Gertrude was aware that the small crowd had not moved on. "Only it's a dead religion."

"My father teaches dead languages."

"He does it at a university. Where would you go to practice a dead religion?"

"Right here. These gods haven't had anybody talking to them for over a thousand years." He looked up at the lofty ceiling.

Somebody chuckled. "Good point."

Gertrude moved closer to him and lowered her voice. "Look, Albert, we've got to call your parents and tell them where you are." She took his arm and whispered, "They've called the police. They're coming to the city."

"I won't go home unless you come, too."

"They don't want me."

"Then I don't go back."

"Why are you so stubborn?" She stamped her foot and the marble made a muffled sound.

After a moment he said, "When I ran away this morning, I didn't know what I was going to do. I thought I'd just come into the city and visit Eddie Fringer and figure out how to find you. I got the Bogueses' number from the telephone book and I called, but somebody I didn't know picked up the phone. I thought it wasn't safe."

Gertrude looked over her shoulder. The small group of people had moved away. "Why did you leave home?"

"It wasn't right that you got punished for the stuff we did together."

"We didn't do 'stuff' together. I did it to you."

"But I let you."

She didn't know how to answer this. "We'll go back to Jessie's and call your parents and explain, or I'll be in even worse trouble with them than I was yesterday."

He stood still and shook his head. "I want to go to your place."

"Nobody's there."

"Do you have a key?"

Gertrude touched it under her blouse. She could see his point. Returning to Jessie's meant a lot of explaining. It might be easier to go to her own apartment and call. They'd be more private. Suddenly she longed to see her own room. She needed to touch her own things and gather strength from them.

A new doorman was in the lobby. He looked at her quizzically.

"I live here," she said.

"What floor?" the doorman called after her.

"My floor," she answered as the elevator door closed on them.

After she had opened the lock with the key she wore around her neck, Gertrude went directly to the kitchen to use the telephone. She turned on the light and took the receiver from the hook. "What's your number, Al?" She hoped her aunt was home by now.

"If you dial it, I'll run right out the door and never come back."

"Your mother is frantic."

"If you call, I'll leave." He turned his back as if to let himself out. "I mean it."

"Okay." Gertrude stalled, hoping for an idea. "Can I phone Jessie? If I don't, her parents will have the police out looking for *me*. I never told them where I was going. They'll be upset."

"What will you say?"

"I'll say that I'm alive and well, and . . ."

"And that you found Albert. No, you can't call them."

"Then I'll just say that I came up to my own place."

"What good would that do? If you call Jessie's house, I'll run out the door."

"Albert, this is crazy. You'll have the state and the city cops on your trail. And for all I know . . ." A thought came to her that caused her to go cold. "For all I know, they'll blame me."

"Why would they do that?"

"Your parents blame me already for making you sick.

They must think it's my fault that you ran away from home. Now if they find out you're with me, maybe I'd get accused of something really serious."

"Like what?" Albert was very interested.

"Like kidnapping."

"I think you're too young. Anyway, I want to be kidnapped." He seemed delighted. "We should stick together. My parents won't really mind. Remember, I'm about to get replaced."

"I was teasing you, Albert."

"I like your place," he said looking around. "I used to think it was peculiar. You have no schedule on the walls. They don't post your papers."

"That's because I don't have any papers."

"I think it's free here," he said, and then he threw back his head and ran in a circle and hooted. "Freee hooooot." When he stopped he fell on the floor. "We had so much fun, Gertie. Remember we played checkers at two o'clock in the morning? When you left the country I had to do Bed Preps and Book Review. When you left, I was all alone again. Boy, we had fun."

"We did?" Gertrude looked at him hard to see if he was kidding. "Getting lost in the woods and punished and having nightmares is your idea of fun?"

He shrugged self-consciously. "Yeah."

Gertrude thought that if that was his idea of fun he was right to run away.

"I'm so hungry I could eat roaches." Albert rubbed

his hands together. "Let's make dinner." He began to open the cupboards. "We'll be like Robinson Crusoe. We'll hunt for food. Nobody will know where we are."

Gertrude looked out the kitchen window into the courtyard. She saw Mrs. Tansey's light switch on and then quickly off again. It was so familiar and pleasant to be in her own place, she couldn't believe she'd been gone for two weeks. Albert was right. It was dinnertime. Kitchen lights were going on up and down the opposite side of the courtyard. Smells of cooking food floated out of the partially opened windows and vents. "There isn't much to eat here. My mother closed down the fridge."

Albert was taking food off the shelves and lining it up on the countertop. "Here's tuna and bread crumbs and soup." He was really enjoying himself. "Hey, Gertie, we're having another adventure." He chuckled and began to joke at the idea. "So You're Running Away from Home — How to Get the Most out of Living without a Daily Schedule. Did I wash my hands? Did I brush my teeth?" He grew serious. "You never had these things, Gertie — that's why I like it here. We could just hole up and watch TV and eat Fritos and drink Funny Face. Nobody would know we were here." He looked around the kitchen. "By the end of the week, all the food would be gone."

"How can you talk about eating and watching TV when I am probably about to go to jail?" Gertrude said dramatically. "Please let me call somebody."

Albert plucked the can opener off its hook on the pegboard and began to open soup and tuna. "We need pots and pans and plates."

"Excuse me." She started for her room.

"Excuse me." He ran behind her. "I know there's an extension in the hall. Remember, I'm not so dumb, Hurdy Gurdy."

"Yes, you are," she hollered, suddenly out of patience.

"If you pick up the phone and I leave and none of you ever find me, it will be your fault. Whatever happens to me will be your fault. You'll be in big trouble."

"I couldn't be in bigger trouble than I am right now."

Since they had been yelling at each other, it took a moment for them to realize that there was a banging at the door and loud voices were calling through it. Gertrude noticed that Albert looked as if he had turned into one of the Roman copies of a Greek marble — "Boy with Can of Tuna." Neither of them could move.

"Open up," a loud voice said through the door. "Police!"

❧ Nineteen ❧

THEY didn't open the door. Instead they ran to the bedroom and crawled under Gertrude's bed, along with the dust balls and the sandals she thought she had lost the summer before. They heard the pounding, and they heard talking and then they heard the key turning in the lock and the sound of the door opening.

"Can we call my parents now?" Albert shuddered. "Can you reach the phone?"

"Do I look like I could reach the phone?" Gertrude was trembling from head to foot.

There were footsteps and voices in the living room. "Come out nice and peaceful. We don't want to hurt anybody. No shooting."

"Shooting?" Gertrude nearly fainted. In the darkness she saw the owls' eyes glint on their shelf. How had she gotten into this?

"Just come out with your hands up."

She crawled out from under the bed, put her arms over her head, and went into the living room. In the middle of the room, in front of the coffee table, were two policemen. Behind them, with his hands on his hips, was Freddy the super, and behind him, bobbing about in her bedroom slippers, was Mrs. Tansey, holding a loop of keys. "Oh no," Mrs. Tansey exclaimed, "it's only Gertie."

"Hey, Gertie," Freddie waved.

"I'm so sorry, officer. I had no idea. I didn't know it was Gertie. Gertie lives here. When I saw the kitchen light go on in the courtyard, you see, my kitchen faces this one, I thought there was a strange-looking boy poking around in the cupboards. I knew the Hollingses were away, you see. They told me they'd be gone three weeks, and this is only two, and they told me to keep an eye on things. I just assumed it was a break-in."

"Where is the boy?" one of the policemen asked Gertrude.

Gertrude opened her mouth to answer, but at the same moment she heard a high strange sound. In a flash Albert more or less flew into the room with his arms out like wings, stiff at his sides, and his head thrust back. "Hooooot," he cried at a piercing pitch, which so astonished everyone that they watched motionless as he whizzed past, through the living room, out the door and down the service steps of the building.

"That was Albert Nugent, Gertie's little cousin," Mrs. Tansey explained to the policemen. "I didn't recognize him through the window."

"Does he think he's a bird?" one policeman asked Gertrude.

"Sometimes," she said.

"We better catch him before he folds his wings," the other policeman suggested, and went out the door after Albert.

"I couldn't feel worse about the whole thing," Mrs. Tansey apologized to Gertrude.

"What were you two kids doing here anyway?" the remaining policeman wondered. "If the place was supposed to be closed up for three weeks. Where are your parents?"

"My parents went to Greece, and I went to Albert's, and then I got kicked out of Albert's, and Albert ran away, and now . . ." She couldn't continue because to her distress she had begun to cry.

"And now he's flown the coop." The policeman was amused.

No one laughed. The elevator clanged shut. To Gertrude's amazement, through her tears she saw Albert (no longer flying) followed by the policeman, who was holding his shoulder, and Mr. and Mrs. Hollings, who were carrying suitcases.

"Gertie." Mrs. Hollings opened her arms.

And Gertrude flew like Olivia into them.

When the two policemen, Mrs. Tansey, and Freddie were gone, Mr. Hollings brought the suitcase into the foyer and closed the door.

"What a homecoming!" Mrs. Hollings collapsed onto the sofa. "Now, tell us the whole story."

"I got into trouble at Eugenia's and was sent away," Gertrude began.

"And I followed her," Albert said.

"And that's the end of the story," Gertrude finished.

"The end of the story?" Mrs. Hollings's brows rose in disbelief. "It can't be."

"End of story," Albert repeated.

Gertrude and Albert exchanged a long look. How could they tell about Owl Games and nightmares and checkers at two o'clock in the morning, and Kition and the dead religion? Those parts were secret. Secrets among themselves.

"I must phone Eugenia." Mrs. Hollings got up. This time Albert did not threaten to fly away.

❧ *Twenty* ❧

WHEN Eugenia and Bruce arrived, Gertrude had the odd sensation that something was happening for the second time.

There were her parents and her aunt and uncle excitedly greeting one another in the foyer as they had only three weeks before. There was Albert standing silently near the door.

"But why did you come home a week early?" Eugenia asked Mrs. Hollings.

"I was sick every morning and couldn't seem to get enough sleep. As soon as the work was finished, I wanted to be home."

Eugenia hugged her. "Do you crave strange foods?"

"I'd love some pickles and pizza."

"That's lucky, because Bruce has ordered a pizza to be sent up for our dinner. Maybe it will be a boy this time." Eugenia turned from her sister and bent to embrace Gertrude. "Oh, Gertie dear, I'm so grateful to you for finding my Albert. How can I thank you enough?"

"Let her come back to Hillside," Albert suggested. "She owes me five games." He tugged at Gertrude's sleeve. "Let's play checkers."

She followed him into her room, as eager as he was to be "alone."

While he set up the pieces, she looked around. There were the stuffed owls on the shelf, the wallpaper and wastebasket and lamp. Her room hadn't changed. But she had a curious feeling that she was a stranger in it. Who was the Gertrude Hollings who lived here? Someone who played with stuffed owls and closed her door to forget as quickly as possible about everything that had happened to her outside this room, this apartment.

"You know, you're getting one, too," Albert said.

"One what?"

"Ennnn ennnnn." He rocked over the board and did an oracle swoon. "A babe who will replace you."

Of course he was right. Why did he always have to figure out everything first? Even when it was something about her own life.

"It's my turn to have the red pieces." Gertrude switched the board around. "You had them last time. You always have them. And I go first."

"Mine will be older and bigger," Albert said.

"Your what?"

"My sibling."

"Yours could be a midget." When she saw Albert twitch, she began to laugh.

At first he looked baffled, but then he began to laugh, too. He pulled the scorecard out of his wallet. "Now watch me win my sixty-seventh game," he said.

"Why not try losing for a change, Al."

"Why should I?" He looked dumbfounded.

"Because for you it would be as hard as flying out of an iron cage right up to the roof and through the window."

"Huh?" Albert's face twitched.

"I dare you to lose." She glared at him.

The phone rang, and Mrs. Hollings called, "It's for you, Gertie."

Jessie said, "Where on earth have you been? We are worried sick."

"Jess, I have so much to tell you."

"This better be good."

"My parents came home. I found Albert. I'm getting a sibling . . ." She was already out of breath.

"Go on . . ."

"Go on? You want more?"

"I'm waiting."

There was a pause during which Gertrude thought they had been disconnected. "Are you there Jessie?"

"I'm thinking."

"What are you thinking?"

"If you're getting a sibling, you will need Sibling Preparation along with the tutorial."

"I do not," Gertrude was adamant. "I've just done S.P. with Albert."

"That doesn't count. You can't do S.P. on yourself," Jessie informed her. "And I don't want to hurt your feelings, but in all honesty, it doesn't sound as if you did such a hot job on him."

"Just a minute." Gertrude heard her voice rise. "It so happens I was a great success."

"Is that why he ran away?"

"He ran away from home because he missed me. I showed him the benefits of being part of a multiple family, of sharing and . . ." She was panting she was so worked up, "and companionship and flexibility." She remembered that this was the list she had been grateful not to have to deal with herself only two weeks ago. She realized that she had dealt with it. She and Albert together. "He followed me because I had established so much respect and rapport that he actually missed me, Jessica Bogues."

There was another pause, during which Jessie could be heard to draw a long breath. "I can't believe it," she exhaled. "Do you realize that I have done it again. My very first consultation, a triumph. We ought to write this up and show it to Mrs. Delson and Godwin's mother. We might get more referrals than we can handle."

Mrs. Hollings called in that the pizza was hot on the table.

"I have to go to dinner, Jess."

"Okay, but bear this in mind. We could be on to something big."

"Could be." Gertrude began to smile. "Anything can happen."

"And I don't mean hair cuts."

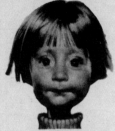

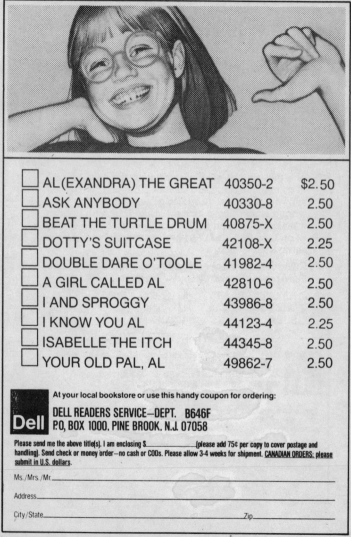